A SNOWBOUND COWBOY ROMANCE

TANISHA POLLARD

Tanisha Pollard

Copyright © 2025 by Tanisha Pollard

ISBN: 979-8-9935159-4-6 (Ebook)

ISBN: 979-8-9935159-3-9 (Paperback

IngramSparks)

ISBN: 979-8-9935159-5-3 (Paperback KDP)

ISBN: 979-8-9935159-2-2 (Hardback)

First Edition: 2025

Tanisha Pollard

Published by: Self-Published

Cover design: Oliviaprodesign.

Interior formatting: Tanisha Pollard

 Content Warnings

While this story is filled with warmth, romance, and holiday magic, it also includes sensitive themes that some readers may find triggering:

❄ PCOS & infertility fears

❄ Medical scenes (surgery, emergencies, hospital environments)

❄ Family criticism & emotional manipulation

❄ Past grief & loss

❄ Alcohol use

❄ High-emotion conflicts & jealousy

❄ Explicit consensual adult intimacy

❄ Winter storm confinement

Your mental well-being matters — please read at your own pace. 🤍❄

Dedication

*For the women who dream of a cowboy who ruins
you gently—*

*with slow hands, sharp desire, and a voice you feel
in your spine.*

For the ones who want to be chosen, chased,

and pulled closer in the quiet glow of firelight.

*For every reader who believes winter is for
surrendering*

to the kind of love that melts you open…

this is yours.

*"Snow or not, sweetheart… I'd still find my way to
you." — Logan Hunter*

Tanisha Pollard

 **Mistletoe Mix-Up Playlist** 

Tennessee Whiskey — Chris Stapleton
Into You — Ariana Grande
Beautiful Crazy — Luke Combs
Earned It — The Weeknd
Love Me Like You Mean It — Kelsea Ballerini
Heaven — Kane Brown
Slow Motion — Trey Songz
Drunk in Love — Beyoncé
Watermelon Moonshine — Lainey Wilson
Love Me Harder — Ariana Grande & The Weeknd
If You Only Knew — Xania Monet
Nonsense — Sabrina Carpenter
Homecoming queen? — Kelsea Ballerini
Forever After All — Luke Combs
All I Want — Kodaline
You Look Like You Love Me — Ella Langley &
Riley Green
All I Want For Christmas Is You — Kelly Clarkson
Santa Tell Me — Ariana Grande
Snowman — Sia

A winter soundtrack for snowy nights, stolen kisses, and the kind of love that sneaks up on you.

Table of Contents

Prologue

Snowflakes slammed against the cabin windows, swirling in the Wyoming dark like a living thing—wild, relentless, impossible to ignore. Avery Collins wrapped both hands around her coffee mug, but the warmth did nothing to steady the storm inside her.

And it had nothing to do with the weather.

It had everything to do with the man standing across the room.

Logan Hunter leaned against the doorway, hat tilted low, boots worn, flannel pulled tight across shoulders that looked built, not shaped. Ink curled just beneath his sleeves—black lines against tan skin that hinted at stories she wasn't brave enough to ask about. He smelled of cedar and cold winter air and something dangerously male, the kind of scent that curled inside her chest and whispered promises she had no business wanting.

"You're staring," he said, voice low enough to heat the space between them.

"I'm not," she lied softly—though her pulse told on her.

He stepped closer. Too close. The crackle of the fire behind him wasn't half as hot as the barely-there brush of his fingers against her jaw. Logan Hunter had a way of looking at a woman that made her imagine things she shouldn't. Things she didn't let herself want.

Especially not now.

Not after the last five years.

The snow howled outside. Inside, her body remembered the way his touch made her knees weaken. And for one terrifying, delicious second, the lie she'd told her family felt dangerously close to the truth she'd never admit out loud.

Chapter 1

Thanksgiving Fallout

Five Years Ago

The clock on the exam room wall ticked far too loudly. Avery sat on the edge of the paper-covered table, wringing her hands as it crinkled beneath her.. The smell of antiseptic filled the air—clean, sharp, unforgiving.

Dr. Reynolds, a middle-aged woman with kind eyes and a clipboard full of numbers, sat across from her. "Avery," she began softly, adjusting her glasses. "I know this isn't what you wanted to hear."

Avery's chest tightened. "You said... something showed up on the ultrasound?"

The doctor nodded, flipping the page to a grainy black-and-white image. "Yes. We found multiple small cysts on your ovaries. Combined with your *hormone levels and symptoms—irregular cycles, hair loss, fatigue—it's consistent with **Polycystic Ovary Syndrome. PCOS.***"

The room seemed to blur around her. "So... what does that mean? Like, for me?"

"It means your body isn't producing hormones in a balanced way," Dr. Reynolds said gently. "It can cause issues with ovulation, weight gain, acne, and sometimes fertility."

Avery blinked hard, trying to process the words that didn't feel real. "Fertility?"

The doctor hesitated, choosing her words carefully. "It doesn't mean you can't have children, Avery. But it may be harder. And the symptoms can affect how you feel physically—and emotionally."

Avery's throat burned. "So, I'm... broken."

"You're not broken," the doctor said quickly, leaning forward. "Your body is just doing what it knows how to do. It's trying to protect you, even if it doesn't feel that way."

Tears welled in Avery's eyes before she could stop them. She looked down, blinking rapidly. "It feels like my body hates me. I do everything right—eat healthy, exercise—but I can't fix this?"

"There's no cure," Dr. Reynolds said softly. "But there are ways to manage it—birth control, medication, diet adjustments, therapy. You're not alone in this."

But Avery didn't hear much after no cure.

When the doctor handed her a pamphlet, she stared at it blankly. The words swam in front of her—hormonal imbalance, infertility, insulin resistance, increased risk of depression.

The tears finally spilled. "I'm twenty," she whispered. "I shouldn't already feel… less than whole."

Dr. Reynolds's expression softened. "You are still you, Avery. This doesn't define you."

But at that moment, it did.

That evening, Avery sat at the kitchen table with her mother, the doctor's pamphlet folded and refolded until the edges tore. The scent of pumpkin pie filled the air, but she couldn't taste or smell anything.

"I just found out today," Avery said, her voice trembling. "It's called PCOS. It explains a lot—why I haven't had a normal period in months, why I've been so tired. I just... wanted you to know."

Her mother frowned, confused. "Is that serious? You don't look sick."

"It's not like that," Avery said quickly. "It's hormonal. It can mess with fertility and—"

Her mother's eyes widened. "Fertility? You mean you can't have kids?"

Avery flinched. "Not exactly. The doctor said it might be harder—"

"Lord," her mother muttered, shaking her head. "I told you all that soda and junk food would catch up. You just don't take care of yourself, Avery. This is why you can't ignore your health."

Avery's chest ached. "It's not my fault."

But her mother had already moved to the phone. "Well, your aunt needs to hear this. Maybe she'll have some advice."

"Mom, no—"

Too late.

By Thanksgiving dinner that weekend, everyone knew.

Her aunt had pulled her into a hug that felt more like pity. "Oh, sweetheart. My friend's daughter had that. She gained so much weight that she couldn't have babies. Poor thing."

Avery froze, eyes darting to her cousins across the table. They whispered and giggled, not even trying to hide it.

"Karma for skipping church."

"No wonder she can't keep a man."

Her uncle laughed. "Or maybe you just need a good man to balance out your hormones."

Laughter erupted around the table.

Avery stared down at her plate, the turkey blurring through tears. She wanted to disappear, to vanish into the tablecloth, to be anywhere but there.

Her mother chuckled lightly, as if to soften the blow. "They're just teasing, honey. Don't take it so personally."

Tanisha Pollard

The sound of their laughter—sharp, careless—stuck to her like oil. She excused herself quietly and slipped into the bathroom, locking the door.

She sank to the cold tile floor, muffling her sobs against her sleeve.

She wasn't angry. Not yet. Just hollow.

*For the first time, she looked at her reflection and didn't recognize herself. Her cheeks were blotchy, her mascara smudged, her body foreign. The pamphlet was still in her bag, the word **"infertility"** bold and unyielding on the page.*

She pressed a trembling hand to her stomach, whispering to herself, "You're not broken. You're not broken."

But deep down, she didn't believe it.

Present Day—Thanksgiving Morning

The operating room was cold, bright, and sterile—the kind of space where emotion had no place. Avery liked it that way. Here, under the hum of fluorescent lights and the steady beeping of monitors, there were no whispers, no judgment. Just precision. Control.

"Scalpel," she said, her voice calm, steady.

The instrument slapped gently into her gloved hand.

She made the incision with practiced ease, the surgical field opening under her touch. Her focus sharpened, blocking out everything else. The chill of the air, the ache in her back, even the faint memory of laughter from five years ago.

This was where she belonged. Where she didn't have to explain herself.

The attending surgeon, Dr. Patel, glanced at her from across the table. "Good form, Dr. Collins. You've got a steady hand."

"Thank you," Avery whispered. Compliments in the OR were rare currency—she tucked it away carefully, like a secret.

They finished the procedure in silence, the patient stable, the rhythm of their teamwork seamless. As Avery sutured the last layer, she felt a small pulse of pride. The girl who once fell apart on a bathroom floor would've never imagined this—being here, confident and capable, the kind of woman who didn't flinch when life turned cold.

When they stepped out of the OR, the hallway was quieter than usual. Most of the staff had taken the holiday off. She stripped off her gloves, dropped them in the bin, and leaned against the counter, staring out the narrow window at the pale November sky.

Snowflakes drifted past the glass—soft, slow, silent.

Her phone buzzed in her pocket.
Mom ♥**:** *Dinner at six. Don't be late this year.*

Avery stared at the message for a long moment. The familiar tightness settled in her chest, the same mix of dread and guilt that always came this time of year. She could already hear her cousins' snide comments, her aunt's not-so-subtle questions about "when she was going to settle down," her mother's nervous laughter when Avery didn't answer fast enough.

She typed a reply, deleted it. Typed again. Deleted that too.

Dr. Patel walked by, coat slung over his arm. "You heading home, Collins?"

"Maybe," she said, forcing a small smile. "Still deciding."

He raised an eyebrow. "You've been on since four a.m. Go. Eat something that doesn't come from the vending machine."

She nodded, but didn't move.

When he left, the hallway fell silent again. Avery looked down at her hands—steady, capable, strong. The same hands that could hold a life steady on the table, yet still shook when she thought about walking through her mother's front door.

Five years later, the diagnosis didn't define her anymore. But the *shame* still lingered.

Outside, the snow thickened—white and unrelenting.

Her phone buzzed with a text from her mom:
The car's waiting. Don't be late this year.

Avery hesitated before replying. Her hand hovered over the screen, heart twisting with that old familiar ache. Going home meant facing *them* again—the whispers, the judgment, the same cutting glances that never really stopped after that day.

But she was older now. Stronger. Or at least, that's what she told herself.

With a deep breath, she tightened her scarf, adjusted her stethoscope necklace—a gift from a grateful patient—and slid into the backseat of the car her parents had sent. The city blurred by, gray and gold in the late autumn light.

Thanksgiving was supposed to be family time. Or at least, that's what her mother insisted.

The ride to her parents' house was quiet, filled with the soft hum of the engine and the crunch of gravel as they turned down the long driveway. Avery's chest tightened the closer they got. She could already hear her family's voices, already feeling the unspoken disappointment waiting for her.

She'd spent the last week on call for multiple emergencies, barely sleeping, and now she had to sit through her family's judgmental eyes as they grilled her about her love life—or lack thereof.

The familiar mix of smells hit her as soon as she walked through the front door: roasted turkey, sage, and a faint trace of her mother's perfume that always made Avery's stomach twist.

"About time you got here," her father said, voice gruff but tinged with humor. "We were thinking your city doctor life had swallowed you whole."

Avery smiled politely. "Traffic was insane." She set her suitcase down and tried to compose herself.

Her mother, ever the picture of perfection, immediately began her inspection. "You're exhausted. Again. Are you really taking care of patients properly if you look like this?"

"I—" Avery started, but her words faltered. She hated lying, hated disappointing her family, but she also hated being criticized for loving her work.

"Doctors work too much," her brother Nate chimed in with a smirk. "You've got an excuse ready, right?"

Avery laughed nervously, brushing a strand of hair from her face. "Something like that."

Her parents exchanged a look. "Something like that?" her mother repeated, eyebrows raised. "Avery, we hardly see you at all. You talk about work like it's your whole life."

"It kind of is," Avery admitted, heart pounding. She wanted them to understand, wanted them to see the good in her choices, but the words caught in her throat.

"And the love life?" her father asked, leaning forward. "Are we ever going to hear about that, or are you too busy saving lives?"

Avery froze. The question had been coming for years, but this time, it felt heavier, more impossible to answer. She swallowed, feeling a surge of panic. She couldn't explain her current complicated dating life—too messy, too exhausting, too unromantic. And after another grueling week in the ER, the thought of another lecture from her family made her heart pound. She needed a solution. Someone authentic enough to play the part. Someone…

"I'm… married," she blurted before she could stop herself.

The room went silent. Utensils hovered midair, eyes wide. Avery's mother almost dropped her fork. Nate grinned wildly, thinking it was a joke.

"Married?" her father's voice was incredulous. "When? Where?"

"I… um… just recently," Avery stammered, wishing the floor would swallow her. "We didn't have a big ceremony… I mean, we didn't really… I just—"

Her brother laughed. "You're joking, right? You can't just drop that on us."

"I'm not," Avery said quickly, panicking, making her voice higher than normal. "We just didn't want anyone to know yet. It's… complicated."

Her parents exchanged a skeptical look, and Avery felt the knot of panic tighten in her chest. How could she fix this? She didn't even know who "he" was—yet. And she certainly didn't have a fake husband ready.

"You expect us to believe that?" her mother asked, arms crossed.

"Yes," Avery said, forcing herself to meet their eyes. "We couldn't wait to be married. Please… just believe me."

Nate leaned back, still smirking. "You've got guts, I'll give you that. But how are we supposed to meet him if he's so… elusive?"

Avery's mind raced. She could see herself losing control over the lie, and the panic made her heart hammer. She needed a solution. She needed someone… real enough to play the part.

She excused herself early, retreating to the guest room under the pretense of exhaustion. Once the door clicked behind her, she sank onto the bed, mind racing. Her phone buzzed—another patient update from the hospital. She stared at it, torn. She wanted to help, as always, but right now she needed someone to help her.

Someone strong. Someone dependable. Someone who could play husband until her family stopped interrogating her.

Somewhere in the back of her mind, she thought of **Logan Hunter.**

Flashback – One Year Ago, Jackson Hole, Wyoming

The air in Jackson Hole was thinner than Avery expected—sharp and clean, carrying the scent of pine and snow. She'd spent the whole morning inside the conference center listening to lectures about surgical technique, her notebook full but her mind restless.

When she finally stepped outside for a break, the late afternoon light painted the mountains in gold. A few blocks down, a small farmers' market was winding down for the day—music playing, boots scuffing against pavement, laughter spilling from a nearby coffee stand.

That's where she saw him.

He stood beside a dark bay horse tied near the fence, cowboy hat tipped low, sleeves rolled up over forearms dusted with sun and ink. He wasn't part of the conference crowd—too rugged, too grounded. The kind of man who looked like he belonged to the land itself.

"Careful," he drawled. "He's friendly, but he steals hearts."

Avery blinked, surprised. "The horse?"

His mouth curved. "Sometimes."

She laughed before she could stop herself. "Smooth line. Does it work often?"

"Only when I mean it." He extended a hand. "Logan Hunter."

Her fingers brushed his—warm, calloused, steady. "Avery Collins."

"Doc, huh?" he said, nodding toward her conference badge still clipped to her coat.

She glanced down and smiled faintly. "You guessed that fast."

"I notice things." His gaze held hers a second too long, the kind of look that made her pulse skip. "You don't strike me as the kind of woman who stays put for long."

"I don't," she admitted. "Life's easier that way."

He tilted his head, studying her. "Easier's not always better."

Something in his tone made her chest tighten. She didn't know this man, not really—but for the first time all week, she felt seen. No small talk, no clinical walls, just something simple and alive sparking between them.

When she finally glanced at her watch, she cursed softly. "I have to get back."

"To your easier life?" he teased.

She smiled, stepping backward. "To my conference."

"Right." His grin deepened. "If you ever get tired of that city pace, there's a whole world out here that runs slower. Quieter."

She hesitated—then said softly, "Maybe I'll take you up on that someday."

He tipped his hat. "You'd better mean it, Doc."

When she walked away, she could still feel his eyes on her, warm against the cold Wyoming air.

And even a year later, when everything unraveled, she still remembered the way his voice sounded when he said her name—steady, certain, like he already knew she'd be hard to forget.

Back in the quiet of her parents' guest room, Avery opened her eyes. The memory lingered, soft but undeniable. Logan Hunter—she hadn't thought about him in months, but now the thought of his calm strength and teasing smile steadied her more than she wanted to admit.

And suddenly, the idea didn't feel so impossible after all.

Chapter 2

No Easy Yes

Avery Collins hated the way her hands shook when she was nervous—right now, they trembled so badly she had to tighten her grip on the steering wheel just to stay on the snow-covered road.

The dashboard cast a faint glow over her warm brown skin, the soft honeyed color standing out against the blue-white chaos outside her windshield. A curl slipped free from her hood, brushing her cheek as she blinked against exhaustion. Her amber eyes reflected equal parts fear and stubborn resolve.

Three hours.

Three hours of nothing but white, pine, and silence.

Three hours to talk herself out of this.

She hadn't.

Because she couldn't.

Her parents' Christmas party was next week, renovations were delaying everything, and—somehow—she had created a husband no one had ever met. What was supposed to be one small lie had become a full-blown expectation.

And now they wanted to meet him.

Only one face came to mind.

Logan Hunter.

She'd met him exactly a year ago at a Jackson Hole medical conference—a place he clearly didn't belong in and didn't pretend to. Avery had bailed on a lecture to grab coffee, half-asleep and praying caffeine would resurrect her.

That's when she saw him by the fence outside:

Sun-browned skin.

Tattoos snaking up both forearms.

A cowboy hat tipped low over wheat-blond hair.

A dark bay horse chewing lazily beside him.

He'd looked like summer heat trapped in the middle of a winter conference.

"Careful," he'd drawled, nodding toward the horse. "He's friendly, but he steals hearts."

She'd laughed—actually laughed—and for five minutes, her world had felt strangely… easy. His blue-green eyes had held hers with a calm curiosity she still remembered. His voice, low and rough, had stuck with her long after she left.

"Easier's not always better," he'd told her.

She'd believed him.

And she'd remembered his name.

Now, snow swirled through her headlights as she pulled up to the ranch she had no business visiting. She rehearsed the words she dreaded saying:

Hi. Remember me? I need you to pretend to be my husband.

The porch light glowed through the storm. Before she could lose her nerve, she climbed out, boots crunching hard against the snow.

She knocked.

Once.

Twice.

And then—

The door swung open.

Logan Hunter stood there, framed by firelight and cold air. His beard was a little fuller, his eyes still that sharp morning-blue rimmed in gray. Tattoos climbed the thick lines of his forearms, disappearing beneath the rolled sleeves of his shirt.

His gaze swept over her slowly, something unreadable flickering behind it.

"Well, I'll be damned," he said, leaning casually against the frame. "Dr. Collins, right? Or was it Avery?"

"Avery's fine," she managed.

"Didn't think I'd see you again," he said. "What brings you out here in a storm like this?"

She swallowed. "I need your help."

He stilled—not shocked, but intrigued.

"Help," he echoed. "You drove three hours for that?"

"Yes."

"Must be important."

"It is."

He stepped aside, letting her in. Warmth wrapped around her instantly—the scent of cedar and smoke, the crackle of fire, the grounding weight of the ranch around her.

Avery turned to him before she chickened out.

"I need you to pretend to be my husband."

The air seemed to freeze.

Logan lifted one brow. "Come again?"

"You heard me," she whispered. "Just for a few days. My family thinks I'm married."

"Why?"

"Because I told them I was."

A low laugh escaped him—amused, not mocking. "Collins, you're somethin' else."

"I didn't think they'd ever want to meet him—meet you—and now they do, and I don't have anyone else who could—"

He cut in softly. "Why me?"

Her cheeks warmed. "Because they'd believe it. You… look the part."

"A rugged cowboy fantasy?" he teased.

"No," she blurted. "Just—someone real. Someone who makes sense."

He studied her long enough that her heart started to stutter.

"You really came all this way to ask me this?"

"Yes," she whispered. "Because I knew you wouldn't laugh."

That stopped him. Completely.

His voice dropped. "You don't know that."

"I do. If you were going to, you would've done it already."

Firelight flickered across his face, softening the edges, deepening the shadows. A breath passed between them, warm and fragile.

"You're askin' for trouble, Collins," he murmured.

"I'm already in trouble. I just need someone beside me while I fake my way through it."

He stepped closer—slow, measured, dangerous.

"I didn't say yes."

"That's not a no."

His mouth curved. "It's not a yes either."

Avery held her breath, pulse thudding painfully in her chest.

She did not know which way he'd lean.

But she knew one thing:

Standing here, wrapped in cedar and firelight and memory, Logan Hunter was the only man alive who could make a lie feel dangerously close to the truth.

Logan — POV

Logan watched Avery Collins standing in the middle of his living room like she didn't belong and somehow fit perfectly at the same time. Snow dusted her hair, her cheeks were flushed from the cold, and those amber eyes—sharp, restless, too honest—held a kind of desperation he hadn't expected.

A fake husband.

Hell of a thing to ask a man you barely knew.

But Logan couldn't ignore the way his pulse kicked up when she said his name again. Or the way the memory of her—laughing at his stupid horse joke a year ago—had stayed tucked somewhere he never admitted to.

She smelled like winter and nerves, and beneath it, something warm. Something real.

He should've said no immediately. He knew that. A woman like her? Danger wrapped in honey. The kind you don't invite into your house if you plan on staying sane.

But the truth dug deeper than he wanted to admit.

He remembered her.

More than he should.

More than was smart.

And now she was back—on his porch, in his house, in his damn space—asking him to play pretend in a way that felt anything but pretend.

Logan scrubbed a hand over his jaw, trying to ignore the tightening in his chest.

Trouble.

That's what she was.

Pure, beautiful trouble.

But as she waited, breath held, he felt a pull low in his gut—one he hadn't felt in a long time.

He didn't have an answer for her yet, not one he trusted himself to say out loud. So instead, he let his voice stay slow, rough.

"Get some rest, Collins," he murmured. "Storm's not letting up anyway."

She blinked, surprised. "Does that mean—?"

"It means," he said, stepping back before he did something stupid, "I'll give you my answer in the morning."

Avery nodded, trying to hide her disappointment. But Logan saw it—felt it—and it did something to him he didn't care to name.

When she walked down the hall toward the guest room, he leaned against the kitchen counter, exhaled hard, and muttered:

"Damn, Doc… what the hell are you pulling me into?"

But even as he said it, he already knew the truth.

He wasn't going to tell her no.

Not then.

Not now.

Maybe not ever.

Chapter 3

Not So Simple

Avery Collins sat on the edge of the couch, hands folded tightly in her lap, staring at the fire. The warmth should have been comforting, but her stomach churned. Logan Hunter leaned against the doorway, arms crossed, boots scuffed and snow-dusted, studying her, like he was trying to solve her

"You really think I'm just going to jump into your little scheme?" he asked, voice teasing, but with a dangerous edge.

"I didn't ask anyone else," Avery said, letting the words rush out before she could second-guess herself. "Because they wouldn't help. My parents wouldn't believe it. You're the only one who could."

He smirked, eyebrow quirked, and took a slow step closer. "The only one, huh? That's quite a compliment."

Avery's cheeks warmed. "It's not a compliment. It's… desperation."

He leaned casually against the table, eyes dark and assessing. "Desperation can be charming… or it can be pathetic. Which are we going for?"

"Neither," she snapped, then immediately regretted her sharp tone. She softened her voice. "I'm serious, Logan. I don't have anyone else. Please, just… consider it."

Logan chuckled, the low, slow kind that made her pulse leap. "Consider it?" he repeated, shaking his head. "You drove three hours in a snowstorm to ask me to play husband. And you want me to just… say yes?"

"Yes," she admitted, voice barely above a whisper. "I need you to say yes."

He stepped closer, tilting his head, and she could feel the heat radiating from him. "You really don't get it, do you? I don't owe you anything, Collins. Nothing."

Avery swallowed hard, trying to steady her voice. "Because I knew you wouldn't laugh at me."

"That's a dangerous assumption," he muttered, his smirk softening just slightly. "You don't know me,

Avery. You barely know me. I don't do favors for strangers."

"I'm not a stranger," she whispered. "And I'm not asking for a favor. I'm asking for your help because you're the only person I can trust to make this believable. And… maybe because I remember you from last year. That coffee shop. You listened when no one else did."

He blinked slowly, his smirk faded for a beat, then returned — teasing, but warmer. "You've got guts, I'll give you that. But I'm not in the habit of walking into someone else's drama just because they flash big brown eyes and beg."

"I'm begging," she admitted, heart hammering. "And yes, you should feel annoyed. You should resist. But please… help me."

Logan leaned against the back of the couch now, close enough that she could feel the faint warmth of his chest. "You know, Collins, you make it hard to say no."

"I don't want easy," she whispered. "I want to be believable. I want… convincing. And I want my family to stop making me feel… small."

There was a silence then, the crackling fire the only sound. Logan's eyes softened as he studied her —

the determination in her expression, the raw honesty she couldn't hide even if she tried. He felt her pain, a pain he himself had recognized.

Finally, he straightened, brushing a hand down his jacket. "Fine," he said, voice low, careful, like he was testing her reaction. "I'll do it. But on my terms."

Avery froze, hope and relief warring inside her. "Your terms?"

"Yeah," he said, with a smirk tugging at his lips. "I get to call the shots. And I get to make it believable. And I get to watch you squirm a little while I do it. Don't think you're getting a free pass just because you begged."

She laughed, a short, nervous sound, but it felt good. "Deal."

He leaned back against the table, eyes twinkling. "And just so we're clear… this doesn't mean we're married. Not really. Just pretend. For your family. And I'm not driving three hours to Cody to live with you. You're coming here for temporary visits. Got it?"

Avery nodded, her pulse still racing. "Got it. Temporary. Pretend. But… believable."

"Exactly," he said, stepping closer and letting his gaze linger on her just a moment too long. "Now, let's see if you can act like a married woman without falling apart under my scrutiny."

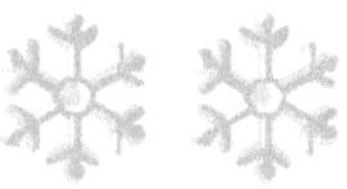

She lay awake long after he'd gone to bed, his words looping in her head. The next morning, Avery woke to the sound of boots on hardwood and the low hum of a country song coming from the kitchen.

 For a moment, she forgot where she was. Then the smell of coffee and bacon hit her, and it all came rushing back.

She sat up on the couch, still wrapped in the thick quilt Logan had tossed over her the night before. He'd offered his guest room, but she hadn't wanted to intrude. Now, looking around the cozy, wood-walled living room, she felt strangely at peace considering she was knee-deep in a lie.

"Morning, city girl," Logan called from the kitchen. "Hope you like your coffee strong enough to wake the dead."

Logan found himself watching her more than he meant to — the way her curls framed her face when she leaned over the counter, or how her eyes caught the firelight, softening from sharp amber to melted honey. She carried herself with quiet certainty, every movement careful, like she'd been trained never to break anything fragile — even hearts.

She stood, tugging her hair into a messy bun. "If it's hot, I'm not complaining."

She glanced up as he entered, wearing a gray T-shirt and jeans that looked far too good on him for someone who claimed not to care about appearances. He slid a mug across the counter toward her.

"Did you sleep okay?"

"Surprisingly, yes," she said, taking a sip. "For someone who might've made the biggest mistake of her life."

He grinned. "You say that like you didn't come up with the idea yourself."

"I thought you'd say no," she muttered.

"Yeah, well." He shrugged, turning back to the skillet. "I was bored."

She laughed under her breath. "You're lying."

He threw her a sideways glance. "Guess that's good practice then, huh?"

Her smile faded slightly. "Practice. Right."

Funny how that word already felt heavier than it should.

Logan turned off the stove and set two plates on the counter, nodding toward the barstool across from him. "If we're going to pull this off, we need to make it believable. You said your family's expecting a husband, not a stranger with a good hat."

She sat curiously. "Okay. What do you suggest?"

"Let's start with the basics." He leaned forward, eyes glinting with challenge. "You're supposed to know me. So—what's my middle name?"

Avery blinked. "I—uh—"

He smirked. "Strike one."

"Fine." She straightened her posture. "What's mine?"

"Elizabeth," he said without hesitation.

Her eyes widened. "How did you—"

"You used your full name when you gave your card at the coffee shop last year," he said, a hint of pride in his tone. "I remember things."

"Okay, cowboy," she said, leaning her elbows on the counter. "What else do I need to know?"

He crossed his arms, pretending to think. "If your mom asks how we met, you say it was at that conference, just like you told me. You spilled coffee on me. I was charming about it, and you fell head over heels."

"I did not spill coffee on you."

"You did in the story," he said, grinning. "It's cute. Women love a meet-cute."

Avery rolled her eyes, but her lips curved. "You're enjoying this way too much."

He leaned closer, the playful smirk never leaving his face. "You're the one who made me your fake husband. Might as well make it entertaining."

She tried not to smile, but it was impossible. "Fine. But if you're going to play my husband, you should probably stop calling me 'Collins.'"

He tilted his head, testing the name on his tongue. "Avery."

Her heart did a funny twist at the sound. She covered it with a sip of coffee. "Better."

"Good. Then I guess we're ready for the next test."

She blinked. "Next test?"

He reached across the counter and took her hand in his — rough and warm and completely unexpected. "Convince me," he whispered. "Make me believe you're my wife."

Avery's breath caught. "How—"

"Look at me," he said.

She did. His blue-gray eyes were steady, challenging but not unkind. She could feel her pulse in her throat, the air between them charged with something neither of them named.

After a long, quiet moment, Logan smiled faintly. "Not bad, Collins."

"I thought you said not to call me that," she whispered.

"Habit," he murmured. "Besides, you blush every time I do."

She pulled her hand back quickly, cheeks burning. "We should… practice more. Talking points. Stories. Details."

"Sure," he said, leaning back with a grin. "But if you blush that easily, you might not have to fake much at all."

She threw a napkin at him, laughing despite herself. "You're insufferable."

"And you," he said, his smile softening, "are in way over your head."

Avery met his gaze, the teasing fading into something deeper. "Maybe. But at least I'm not alone."

Logan's expression flickered — something unspoken passing between them before he looked away, clearing his throat. "Eat your breakfast, Collins. We've got a fake marriage to plan."

Chapter 4

Unexpected Guests

The hospital smelled of antiseptic and fatigue, a mix Avery knew too well. She moved through it like muscle memory—gloves snapping, monitors chirping, her mind staying sharp even as the edges of exhaustion tugged at her. Handling emergencies was easy. Handling her mother's holiday plans was… something else entirely.

Her phone buzzed across the counter. *Mom* .

Avery winced before she even pressed play.

"Dr. Collins? Everything okay?" Dr. Patel called as he passed.

"Fine," Avery lied smoothly. "Just… holiday chaos."

She put the phone on speaker and braced herself.

Her mother's overly bright voice filled the room:

"Sweetheart! Wonderful news! Since the renovations will run through Christmas, your father

and I thought—why not spend the whole month with you and your new husband? We can bake, decorate, and really get to know Logan!"

Avery blinked. Once. Twice.

The entire month? On the ranch? With Logan?

Her stomach hit the floor.

The moment she caught a break between surgeries, she ducked into a quiet hallway and FaceTimed him. Her pulse thudded in her throat as she waited.

Logan answered on the second ring, the screen filling with his rugged face and the soft glow of his cabin behind him. "Morning, Collins," he drawled. "Storm bad enough that you're calling this early?"

"Worse," she said, breath shaky. "Mom called."

One of his eyebrows lifted. "That bad, huh?"

"She wants to spend the whole month of December at your ranch. All of them. My entire family." Avery swallowed. "Logan… she thinks we're living together. Married. Blissful."

There was a beat of silence.

Then—

"The entire month?" His voice dropped, low and incredulous. "Avery… Do you have any idea what you're asking?"

She winced. "Yes. And no. And also yes."

"Collins," he muttered, running a hand over his jaw. "Your family—your holiday family—at my ranch? For four weeks?" He let out a humorless laugh. "I'm not exactly the warm-and-fuzzy type."

"I know." She took a breath. "But we agreed to pretend. This is part of it. I can't tell them the truth. Not now."

He didn't answer at first. She heard the faint crackle of his fire, the muffled whistle of wind hitting his cabin walls.

"You're asking for trouble," he finally said.

"I'm already in trouble," she whispered. "I just… I need you, Logan."

His jaw flexed, the movement subtle but sharp.

Then he sighed, long and slow. "Fine. I'll do it. But—your family follows my rules. My ranch, my boundaries. And if your aunt tries to rope me into cookie decorating… I'm out."

Avery laughed, the relief so fierce it nearly made her dizzy. "Deal. Thank you."

"Don't thank me," he muttered, though she could see a smirk tugging at his mouth. "Save it for when the snow traps all of us and your brother tries riding one of my horses."

"Okay, that one… could actually happen," she admitted.

He groaned. "Fantastic."

By the end of her shift, Avery's back ached and her mind spun. All she could think about was the month ahead—thirty-one days of faking romance with a man who already made her pulse misbehave. Thirty-one days of her family in close range. Thirty-one days of trying not to want what she absolutely shouldn't.

That night, headlights cut through the snow as she pulled up to Hunter Ranch. The air hit her like ice, cold enough to sting her cheeks. Snow crunched under her boots as she climbed the steps, breath turning to fog in the glow of the porch light.

Inside, the cabin warmth wrapped around her instantly—cedar, firewood, and something unmistakably Logan. He stood by the hearth, coffee mug in hand, firelight carving shadows along his jaw.

He didn't look at her when he spoke. "So… the Collins Christmas circus is officially coming to town."

Avery flinched. "One way to put it."

He finally met her eyes, the corner of his mouth lifting. "You're lucky I'm in a generous mood."

"Generous?" She set her bag down. "You nearly bit my head off earlier."

"You're pushy," he said simply. "But I respect that."

She folded her arms. "So… we're doing this? For real?"

He nodded. "For real. But we need rules."

On the table, he had a notepad scribbled with a list.

1. How we met: keep the story simple—conference last year.

2. PDA only when necessary.

***3.** No family member gets free rein in my barn.*

***4.** You handle the decorating. I'll pretend to care.*

***5.** If asked why we don't live together—blame work.*

Avery raised an eyebrow. "Rule five seems a little too accurate."

"Exactly," he said.

For a moment, the world slowed. The fire popped. Wind brushed the windows. She couldn't tell where the warmth was coming from—the hearth or him.

"Logan?" she said softly.

"Yeah?"

"Thanks. Really."

His gaze held hers—steady, unreadable, a little dangerous.

"Don't thank me yet, Collins," he murmured. "We haven't even hit mistletoe season."

Later, lying in the guest room, Avery stared at the ceiling as wind rattled the cabin. She'd survived trauma rooms, impossible patients, and her mother's scrutiny.

But nothing—absolutely nothing—could prepare her for pretending to be married to a man like Logan Hunter.

And something told her that by Christmas morning…

Neither of them would be pretending anymore.

Logan — POV

Logan Hunter wasn't a man who rattled easily.

Ranch work didn't leave much room for panic—cold mornings, stubborn cattle, busted fences, he could handle all of it without breaking stride. But this?

This was different.

He stood in the dim hallway outside the guest room, mug still warm in his hand, listening to the storm push against the cabin walls. Avery Collins—Avery with her sharp tongue, steady hands, and eyes that could cut through a man if he wasn't careful—was lying just feet away. In his house. In his life.

Hell.

He scrubbed a hand over his jaw, staring at the snow piling up outside the window. He should've said no. Should've told her she was out of her mind, driving through a storm and barging into his world like she didn't know the chaos she carried with her.

But the truth was, he remembered her.

More than he wanted to admit.

Those five minutes a year ago hadn't slipped out of his head the way they were supposed to. The way most people faded. Something about her had stuck—her stubbornness, the way she kept her guard up even when she smiled. The way she'd looked at him like she was trying to memorize him but didn't want him to notice.

And tonight, seeing her standing in his doorway with snow in her hair and panic in her eyes…

Yeah. He never really stood a chance.

Avery Collins needed help. And even if he pretended otherwise, he'd already made up his mind before she finished the words I need you.

What bothered him wasn't the lie.

He could fake a lot of things.

What bothered him was how damn real it had felt watching her unpack her nerves and trust him with them. Like she didn't know how dangerous it was to lean on a man like him. Like she didn't know that once he let someone into his space—his quiet, his routines, his home—they didn't get to leave without taking something of him with them.

He cursed under his breath, finishing his coffee.

A month.

An entire month of her family taking over his ranch.

An entire month of sleeping under the same roof, pretending to be her husband, answering questions, touching her shoulder, her waist, her hand, whenever people were watching.

Pretending.

Right.

He didn't believe that for a damn second.

Not after seeing how she looked at him. Not after feeling the way the air tightened between them when she said his name.

Logan leaned against the wall and let the truth settle, heavy and unwelcome but impossible to ignore:

He wasn't worried about lying to her family.

He was worried about what would happen when the lie started feeling better than the truth.

He blew out a slow breath and shook his head.

"Trouble," he muttered to the empty hallway. "That woman is pure trouble."

And somehow, without meaning to—

he already knew he'd walk straight into it.

Chapter 5

Snow, Secrets, & Small Fires

The morning sunlight filtered through the cabin windows, spilling gold across the rough-hewn floorboards. Avery sipped her coffee, eyes fixed on the snowy expanse outside. Her laptop hummed beside her, filled with patient charts she was supposed to be ignoring.

"You really don't know how to relax, do you?"

Logan's voice came from the doorway, low and teasing. He stood with one shoulder braced against the frame, his flannel sleeves rolled to the elbows, dark hair mussed from the wind.

"I can relax," she said, though her tone made it sound more like a defense than a truth. "Just not yet. My patients rely on me."

He crossed the room; the floor creaking under his boots. "You're supposed to be spending the holidays pretending to be my wife, remember?" His smirk deepened. "Not pretending to run a hospital from my kitchen."

Avery looked up at him, arching a brow. "Maybe I can multitask."

"Or maybe," he murmured, leaning close enough for her pulse to skip, "you're scared to stop working because then you'll actually have to be here—with me."

Her breath caught. She opened her mouth to respond, but before she could, the sound of tires crunching over snow sliced through the quiet. Her heart jumped.

"They're here," she whispered.

Logan straightened, with a low groan rumbling in his chest. "Lord help us."

Avery's stomach twisted as she set her mug down and smoothed her sweater. "Okay, we practiced this—sort of. Just… act normal."

"Normal?" he echoed, reaching for his hat. "Collins, you dragged me into a Christmas-long lie. There's nothing normal about this."

Before she could argue, the front door burst open, and a rush of cold air followed her family inside.

Her mother, as elegant as ever, arrived in a cream coat and scarf. Her skin was a few shades darker than hers, smooth and radiant even in the cold, her curls tucked beneath a knitted hat. Her father's beard had gone silver around the edges, but his laugh was the same as Avery's — bright and warm enough to fill a room. Even her brother, tall and broad-shouldered, carried the same golden undertone in his skin and that familiar glint of mischief in his eyes. The luggage was carried by her father. Her grandmother and brother, Nate, trailed behind with a grin that could only mean trouble.

"Oh, sweetheart!" her mother exclaimed, pulling Avery into a hug. "This place is… rustic."

"Rustic," Logan repeated dryly, tipping his hat. "I'll take that as a compliment, ma'am."

Her mother blinked at him, then smiled too brightly. "You must be Logan! I've heard so much about you."

"I doubt that," he said, voice smooth as whiskey. "But I'll try to live up to the stories."

Avery shot him a warning glance, but he only smirked and offered to take her mother's coat. Her father's firm handshake followed, and then came Nate's raised brow.

"So this is the mysterious cowboy," he said, eyeing Logan's boots. "Didn't think you had it in you, sis."

Avery forced a laugh. "Guess I surprised you."

Logan's hand slid around her waist—steady, confident. "She surprises me every day," he said smoothly, kissing her temple, and Avery nearly forgot to breathe.

As her family settled themselves in the living room, Logan pulled her to the side. Avery froze at his touch, but Logan didn't miss a beat. He reached into his pocket, pulling out a small velvet box. "Almost forgot this," he murmured, flipping it open with one hand. Inside sat a delicate gold band, simple but elegant.

Avery's breath hitched. "Logan—"

"Play along," he whispered in her ear, so quietly only she could hear. "I thought, since we need to be believable, I would take the initiative."

He slid the ring onto her finger, his thumb brushing her skin. The touch sent a shiver through her.

As they headed back to the living room, her mother enveloped her in another hug. Her mother's eyes then flicked down to her hand. "Oh! The ring!"

"Perfect fit," her mother gushed. "How romantic!"

"Couldn't wait to make it official," Logan said, eyes never leaving Avery's. "Didn't see the point in waiting once I knew she was the one."

Her heart stuttered. He was acting, of course—but it didn't *feel* like acting.

By afternoon, chaos had settled into the cabin like a second skin. Decorations in boxes lay scattered across the living room. Nate and Logan were stringing lights along the mantle, both pretending not to compete over who could make them straighter.

Avery's mother busied herself in the kitchen, humming Christmas tunes and "supervising" every detail. Her father was outside admiring the barn, muttering something about "proper country living."

Avery tried to juggle conversation, decorations, and her laptop alerts, but Logan's presence was impossible to ignore. Every time he passed her—his hand grazing her back, eyes lingering a beat too long—her pulse tripped over itself.

"Everything okay, *Mrs. Hunter*?" he asked quietly, leaning close as he fixed a crooked garland.

She shot him a glare. "You're enjoying this too much."

"Maybe," he said, smirking. "You make it easy."

Later, while her family took a walk around the snowy property, Avery found Logan splitting wood by the barn. His movements were smooth, powerful—each swing measured and precise.

"You handled them better than I expected," she said, stepping closer, boots crunching in the snow.

He looked up, wiping his brow. "I've handled cattle stampedes quieter than your family."

She laughed, the sound echoing in the cold air. "I owe you for this."

"Damn right you do." He leaned the axe against the stump, gaze softening. "But I'll admit—seeing you smile like that today… maybe this isn't the worst idea."

Her laughter faded, replaced by something quieter. Warmer. "You didn't hate it?"

"I didn't say that," he murmured. "I just didn't hate all of it."

That night, the storm rolled in, thick and relentless. Snow fell in heavy sheets, trapping them inside. The fire glowed low and steady, painting gold across Logan's face as he lounged on the couch beside her.

Her family's laughter drifted faintly from the guest cabins outside, muffled by the wind.

Logan leaned closer, his voice low. "You did well today."

"So did you," she whispered, unable to stop staring at him.

He smiled, small and slow. "Don't get used to it."

Their eyes held, the fire crackled, and for one dizzying heartbeat, the line between pretend and real disappeared completely.

The world outside was still ink-dark when Avery's phone buzzed somewhere near her pillow. She groaned, fumbling for it, but the sound that finally woke her wasn't the alarm—it was the low thud of boots on the porch and the distant rattle of a feed bucket.

Through the window, a faint glow burned across the horizon. The ranch was already alive. The air carried that sharp mix of hay, diesel, and cold iron she'd only ever smelled on him—hard work, distilled into scent.

She tugged on her coat and stepped outside, the cold biting her cheeks. Logan was in the corral, breath fogging in the dawn air, scattering grain for the chickens. A rooster crowed once—late, indignant.

"You ever sleep?" she called, her voice muffled by the scarf.

He looked over his shoulder, smirking beneath the brim of his hat.

The early light carved every line of him into definition — the kind of strength built from years of lifting hay bales and fixing fences. His skin was tanned deep bronze, kissed by both sun and wind, and faint scars traced stories along his forearms. Tattoos swirled up his skin like shadows under gold, and when he smiled, the dimple at the edge of his jaw deepened — the same place a faint white scar caught the light.

"Not much. Ranch doesn't care if I'm tired. Chickens need feed, horses need water, fences need fixin'. That's before breakfast."

Avery crossed her arms, watching him move. Each motion was precise, practiced—he worked like a man who'd done this a thousand mornings and still loved it.
"You start all this before sunrise?"

"'Round three or four," he said, straightening. "Get the hard stuff done before the sun decides to bake you alive—or freeze you solid."

She laughed softly. "City people call that insanity."

He leaned on the fence, eyes glinting. "Out here we call it discipline."

The sky blushed pale pink as he led her toward the barn. The scent of hay, diesel, and frost mingled in the air. Inside, heat and light wrapped around them—the rhythmic hum of a tractor, horses shifting in their stalls, a radio murmuring an old country song. His sleeves were dusted with hay, the cuff of his flannel damp from morning dew, every inch of him proof that he'd already lived a full day before sunrise.

"Cotton, corn, rye, and greens," he said, nodding toward the distant fields beyond the frosted glass. "Each one's got its own season. You prep the soil, plant, and pray the weather doesn't turn mean. If there's a drought, we wait. You can't force the land—it teaches patience." She realized he talked about the soil the way she talked about medicine—precise, patient, reverent. Both of them learning where control ends and faith begins.

She studied him quietly. The way he spoke about the earth wasn't small talk; it was faith. "You really love it here."

"My papaw used to say the land don't owe you a damn thing," he said, glancing toward the fields. "You just show up every day, do right by it, and hope it gives back enough to keep you fed. He's the one who taught me all this—how to fix a busted fence, calm a horse, tell when the ground's ready to plant. He was up by three every morning, had breakfast on by five, and still found time to haul me to town for coffee after chores.
 He'd say, *'Work hard enough, and the land'll remember your hands.'*"

Avery smiled softly. "You miss him."

"Every damn day," Logan admitted quietly. "Papaw's why I'm still here. This ranch is his heartbeat. I'm just keepin' it steady."

Logan shrugged, though his voice softened. "It's honest work. Land gives what you give it. Same with people—most of the time."

Their eyes met. The words hung there, heavier than they should have.

He turned first, grabbing a bale of hay and hoisting it into a stall with effortless strength. "If you're gonna pretend to be my wife, Doc, you might as well learn how to stack feed without lookin' like it's gonna bite you."

"Excuse me?" she said, but he was already grinning.

"Grab the other end," he teased.

The bale was heavier than it looked. She stumbled, nearly losing her balance, and his hand shot out, steadying her at the waist. For a moment, neither moved. His glove brushed her coat, warm and solid, and the world narrowed to the steady sound of their breathing.

"Careful," he murmured, voice low. "You'll make me think you like this."

Avery forced a laugh, stepping back. "Maybe I just don't want to fall on my face."

He tilted his hat, eyes lingering a heartbeat longer than necessary. "Whatever helps you sleep tonight."

They finished the chores together—she fetched buckets, he lifted the heavy work. By the time the first true light spilled across the pasture, her cheeks were flushed and her heartbeat strangely light.

When they reached the porch again, Logan handed her a steaming mug of coffee. "You did good for a city girl," he said, a grin tugging at his lips. "Didn't complain once."

"Was I supposed to?"

"Most would've. You didn't."

The compliment was quiet, sincere. It settled somewhere deep, warming her more than the coffee ever could.

Above them, gray clouds gathered on the horizon, thick and heavy with snow. Logan followed her gaze.
 "Storm's comin'," he said. "You'll wanna stay close to the fire tonight."

Avery smiled faintly. "I think I can manage that."

He looked at her for a long moment, the kind of look that saw too much. "Yeah," he said finally, voice soft. "I bet you can."

The wind picked up, scattering a few stray feathers across the yard. The first flakes began to fall.

By nightfall, the storm would trap them inside. But for now—just for this breath of morning—Avery felt something new stirring in her chest. Not fear. Not panic.

Something alive.

Chapter 6

Snowstorm Brewing

The snow fell relentlessly, blanketing the ranch in a hushed white silence. Outside, the wind howled against the cabin walls, rattling the windows like a warning. Inside, Avery stirred the stew on the stove, the scent of rosemary and smoke filling the air.

She glanced at her phone again—another patient alert. Another urgent case she couldn't reach. The storm had knocked out most of the signal, leaving her stranded in more ways than one.

Logan leaned against the counter, arms crossed, his boots dusted with snow, watching her with that steady, unreadable gaze.

"You're still working," he said, voice low, teasing—but with an edge of something else. Concern. Maybe frustration.

"I'm trying," she murmured, brushing a loose strand of hair behind her ear. "My patients don't wait for snowstorms, but unfortunately I can't get to them right now. Other things can wait."

He smirked, stepping closer. "Some things can wait," he whispered, his voice rough with something she couldn't quite name. "Like… us."

Her breath caught. "Us?"

He didn't answer, just reached for the spoon beside her. His fingers brushed hers—light, deliberate. The touch lingered just long enough to send a shiver racing through her.

"I know you're doing your job," he said finally, his tone softer now. "But I enjoy having you here. When you're not buried behind that laptop."

Her cheeks warmed despite herself. She wanted to say something clever, something to break the tension, but the words tangled in her throat.

Outside, the wind picked up, snow swirling higher. Avery glanced at the frosted window. "Looks like we're snowed in."

"Guess that means I've got your undivided attention," Logan said, his grin slow and dangerous.

She turned back to the pot, pretending to focus. "You wish."

"Oh, I don't need to wish," he said, brushing past her to grab a mug. "You'll crack before I do."

The afternoon slipped by in a haze of chores and stolen glances. Avery chopped vegetables while Logan stacked firewood, their quiet rhythm laced with an easy intimacy. Every time their hands brushed—passing a plate, a towel, a spoon—the charge between them deepened.

By evening, the storm roared outside, sealing them in completely. The world beyond the cabin had vanished—just snow, wind, and the steady hum of tension neither wanted to name.

Avery retreated to her laptop, catching a flicker of signal long enough to send an update to the hospital. She sighed, shoulders tight, when Logan appeared in the doorway, shadowed by firelight.

"You're going to work yourself to exhaustion," he whispered, voice lower now, almost coaxing. "And I will not let that happen."

"I can't just ignore it," she said, though her voice lacked conviction.

He crossed the small room, holding out a mug of cocoa. "Then at least take a break."

Their fingers brushed as she took it, warmth spreading through her palms—and somewhere deeper.

They sat side by side near the fire; the storm raging against the walls and the flames crackling in a quiet rhythm. Silence stretched between them, heavy and charged.

"I can't…" Avery began, voice trembling. "I can't let this go too far."

Logan's hand found hers, fingers twining effortlessly, as if it had always been that way. "Pretend or not," he breathed, his eyes dark and steady on hers, "being near you feels too real to fight."

The wind howled outside, snow burying the world beyond their walls, but inside, heat rolled between them like a living thing. Avery's pulse pounded as she realized—whatever this was, whatever they were pretending—it was already blurring into something neither of them could walk away from.

By morning, the storm showed no mercy. Snow drifts climbed high against the porch, the fences half-buried under a thick white blanket. The main house was quiet—too quiet. Avery knew that wouldn't last long.

From the hall came her mother's voice, bright and commanding as ever. "Logan, dear! Will we be stuck here all weekend because of this storm?"

Logan, still in his flannel and jeans, leaned against the counter, coffee in hand. "Depends," he said evenly, his deep voice carrying just enough dry humor. "If it keeps up like this, maybe through Christmas."

Her mother gasped, half in horror, half in delight. "Oh! A real white Christmas! Isn't that wonderful, Avery?"

Avery forced a smile. "So wonderful," she said, deadpan.

Nate stumbled in next, half-asleep, muttering about no cell service and terrible coffee. Grandma Collins followed, wrapped in a shawl, mumbling something about "ranch living" and "city girls making poor choices."

Avery sighed and shot Logan an apologetic look. He only smirked, clearly amused by her family's morning invasion.

When her mother started rearranging the Christmas décor *again* — this time suggesting Logan's mounted antlers would "look festive with garland"—Avery caught his jaw tighten ever so slightly.

"Careful," she whispered when they crossed paths in the kitchen. "You look like you're two minutes from losing it."

He leaned close, voice low so only she could hear. "Your mother just told me my coffee tastes like mud."

"She's not wrong," Avery said, biting back a laugh.

"You never complained before?" he said.

"Well, that's because you're doing this big thing for me, sooo…." she giggled.

Logan's gaze darkened. "You're lucky I like you, Collins."

The day wore on in a blur of chaos. Nate offered to "help" with chores, only to get chased by one horse. Her grandmother complained about the cold draft by the fireplace. Her mother baked enough cookies to feed the entire county—and somehow managed to critique Avery's marriage while frosting them.

Through it all, Logan moved like a quiet storm—steady, stoic, and only slightly murderous. But every time Avery caught his eye, there was that glint again. Amusement. Interest. Heat.

By evening, the storm had intensified, rattling the windows as darkness fell. The family had retired to the guest cabin, leaving Avery and Logan alone in the main cabin.

Avery sat near the fire, legs tucked under her blanket, scrolling through patient charts she couldn't update. Logan dropped onto the couch beside her, the cushion dipping under his weight.

"Busy saving lives again?" he asked, eyes glinting in the firelight.

"Trying to," she mumbled. "The signal's gone again."

He leaned in, voice low. "Guess that means you're stuck with me."

Her pulse kicked up; the warmth from the fire was nothing compared to the heat that pooled in her chest. "You make that sound like a bad thing."

"Never said it was," he murmured.

For a moment, the storm outside seemed to fade. It was just them—close, unguarded, pretending a little less with every breath.

Then, from the hall, her mother's voice cut through the air. "Avery, dear! Could you bring more firewood before bed? And maybe ask Logan to show you how to use that old stove? It's *so romantic*!"

Avery groaned, burying her face in her hands. "She's never going to stop, is she?"

Logan chuckled, the sound low and rich. "Not a chance. But… she's not wrong."

Avery lifted her head, narrowing her eyes. "About what?"

He gave her a half-smile, the slow, infuriating kind that made her heartbeat stutter. "The romantic part."

The silence that followed was anything but quiet. The wind howled outside; the fire popped and hissed, and Avery held her breath.

Pretend or not, she was falling—and she knew he felt it too.

The wind howled louder as the night deepened, slamming against the windows as if it wanted in. The fire crackled low, throwing soft amber light across the cabin walls. Avery had tried going to her room twice, but each time the cold bite was sharper, the power flickered longer, and the silence grew heavier.

On the third outage, she gave up.

"Generator's out," Logan said, reentering the room with a flashlight and two heavy blankets draped over his arm. "The furnace won't kick back on until it does."

"Perfect," Avery muttered, rubbing her hands together. "Freezing to death in Wyoming—what every doctor dreams of."

Logan chuckled, setting one blanket over her shoulders. "You won't freeze. Not on my watch."

The way he said it—quiet, certain—made her pulse jump.

She watched him move around the cabin, checking the fire, sealing the window latch, every motion slow and steady, controlled. He'd changed into a gray thermal shirt and joggers, and the sight of him barefoot by the fire shouldn't have been distracting, but somehow, it was.

When he finally sank down beside her, close enough for their knees to brush, Avery realized the warmth between them was far more dangerous than the storm outside.

"Looks like we're camping in the living room," Logan said, nodding to the couch and the pile of blankets. "The guest rooms will be colder than a freezer tonight."

Avery hesitated. "You mean… we're both sleeping here?"

He gave her that half-smile again. "Unless you'd rather risk hypothermia."

"Fine," she said, trying for nonchalance even as her heart raced. "But I'm taking the couch."

"Suit yourself," he murmured, spreading his blanket on the rug by the fire.

Minutes passed. The flames dimmed, the storm outside roared, and Avery shivered despite the blanket wrapped around her.

Logan noticed. "You're freezing."

"I'm fine."

He arched his eyebrow. "You're *stubborn.*"

Before she could argue, he rose, grabbed his blanket, and dropped it over both of them, settling beside her on the couch. Their shoulders brushed, his warmth immediate, grounding.

"Better?" he asked softly.

She exhaled, tension slowly easing. "Yeah. Better."

For a long while, neither spoke. The firelight painted his face in gold and shadow, his eyes soft when they drifted to her.

"Do you ever tire of pretending?" he asked suddenly, voice barely above a whisper.

She blinked, surprised. "Pretending?"

"This whole thing—smiling when you're worn down, keeping it together when everyone expects you to."

Avery's throat tightened. "Every day."

He nodded slowly, gaze dropping to the fire. "Guess we're both good at playing parts."

Something in his tone tugged at her—an honesty that felt too raw to ignore. Without thinking, she reached for his hand beneath the blanket. Warm. Calloused. Solid.

"Maybe," she said quietly, "we don't have to pretend tonight."

Logan's head turned toward her, eyes searching hers. The storm raged harder outside, snow thrashing against the glass. Inside, everything stilled—every sound swallowed by the slow, uneven rhythm of two hearts finding sync.

He didn't move closer. He didn't need to. Their feelings expressed themselves through the charged air between them.

After a long moment, he squeezed her hand once, gently but surely. "Get some sleep, Doc."

She smiled faintly, closing her eyes as her head tipped against his shoulder.

Outside, the storm showed no sign of stopping;
inside, neither did whatever was quietly building
between them.

Chapter 7

Too Close For Comfort

Sunlight spilled weakly through the frost-rimmed window, pale and hesitant after the storm's long night. The embers of the fire had died down, and a sleepy stillness wrapped the cabin, making the world outside feel a million miles away.

Avery stirred first. Her cheek rested against something solid and warm—definitely not a pillow.

Her eyes fluttered open.

Logan.

He was still asleep, head tipped back against the couch, arm wrapped protectively around her shoulders as if keeping her there. His chest rose and fell in a peaceful rhythm, the early light tracing the line of his jaw and the faint scruff along it.

For one dizzy, unguarded moment, Avery didn't move. She just… watched him. The way his expression softened in sleep, the way his fingers were still loosely tangled with hers beneath the blanket.

And then it hit her.

Oh no.

She sat up too fast, bumping his shoulder. Logan grunted, blinking awake. "What time is it?"

"Too early for this," she whispered, heart thudding.

He rubbed his eyes, gaze finally focusing on her—and the close space between them. A slow, teasing grin spread across his face. "Well… good morning, wife."

She groaned, burying her face in her hands. "Don't start."

But before he could reply, the sound of footsteps echoed down the hallway.

Avery froze. "Oh no, oh no, oh no—"

Logan barely had time to sit up before her mother's voice called out, chipper and unsuspecting. "Sweetheart? Are you up? I made pancakes!"

The door creaked open, and there stood her mother—bright smile, festive sweater, and a tray of breakfast in her hands. Her gaze fell instantly on the couch. On Avery. On Logan. Upon the shared blanket.

For a moment, no one moved.

Then came the slow, knowing smile. "Well," her mother said cheerfully, "looks like the honeymoon phase is going just fine."

Avery's jaw dropped. "It's not what it looks like!"

Logan leaned back, a smirk tugging at his lips. "Sure it isn't."

Her mother laughed softly, setting the tray on the coffee table. "Breakfast for the newlyweds. Don't get up too quickly—you two look… cozy."

When she left, Avery groaned again, pulling the blanket over her face. "I can't believe this."

"Oh, I can," Logan said, tone infuriatingly calm as he reached for a pancake. "If I didn't know better, I'd say the storm did me a favor."

She shot him a glare, cheeks blazing. "You are impossible."

"Maybe," he said, his grin softening just a little, "but admit it—this fake marriage is getting real complicated."

Avery crossed her arms, fighting a smile she didn't want him to see. "You have no idea."

Sunlight glittered across the snow-covered fields outside, as if someone had scrubbed the world clean overnight. Inside the cabin, however, nothing felt simple anymore—not after that storm, not after that night, and definitely not after the look Logan gave her when he thought she wasn't watching.

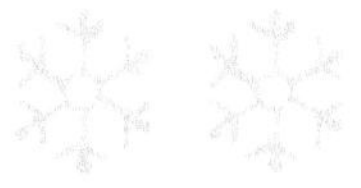

By the time Avery and Logan made it to the kitchen, the smell of cinnamon and coffee filled the air. Her mother was already bustling between the stove and the counter, humming along to some old holiday song while her aunt set the table.

Her brother, Nate, sat at the end of the table with a mug of coffee, grinning like he'd just uncovered the world's greatest secret.

"Well, well, look who finally rolled out of bed," he said, smirking. "Sleep well, lovebirds?"

Avery stopped short, color flooding her cheeks. "Nate—"

But Logan, of course, didn't miss a beat. "Like a rock," he said easily, reaching for a plate. "Didn't even notice the storm."

Her brother nearly spit out his coffee laughing. "Oh, man. You're good."

Avery glared at both of them. "You two are insufferable."

"Sweetheart, don't tease them," her mother said, setting down a plate piled high with pancakes. "Let them enjoy their first married Christmas together."

Avery wanted to crawl under the table. "Mom, please—"

Logan just smiled, the picture of calm confidence. "I'm enjoying it plenty, ma'am."

Her grandma winked. "I bet you are, cowboy."

Avery groaned and sank into her seat, wishing the floor would swallow her whole. Logan only chuckled, his knee brushing hers under the table. The casual contact shouldn't have meant anything, but her pulse jumped all the same.

"So, Logan," her mother began as she poured coffee. "How's life on the ranch treating my daughter? She hasn't scared off the horses yet, has she?"

"Not yet," he said with a grin. "But she's trying her best."

Her grandmother laughed. "Oh, that sounds just like Avery."

"I heard that," Avery muttered, stabbing a piece of pancake.

Nate leaned back in his chair, watching the two of them closely. "You know," he said slowly, "I wasn't sure about you, Logan. But I've got to say—you handle my sister pretty well. Most men wouldn't last a week."

Logan met his gaze, a flicker of amusement in his eyes. "I don't scare easily."

"Oh, he's perfect," her mother said dreamily. "Strong, polite, handy, and patient. Avery, darling, where did you find him again?"

Avery froze. "Um—well, it's kind of a long story—"

"She ran into me," Logan said smoothly, his voice warm but deliberate. "Literally. Outside a feed store."

Her mother clasped her hands. "Oh, how romantic!"

Avery blinked at him. That wasn't true. It wasn't even close. But as her mother beamed, and her brother grinned, she couldn't find it in herself to correct him.

Logan's gaze met hers across the table, steady and full of quiet mischief.

And in that moment, with her family laughing and the snow glittering outside the window, Avery realized just how dangerous this was becoming. The lie wasn't just convincing to her family—it was convincing to her.

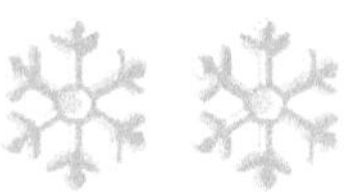

After the table was cleared and her family dispersed—her mother humming in the kitchen, her aunt cooing over Christmas decorations, and Nate off to "help" with the horses—Avery put on her coat and went out.

The air was sharp, biting at her cheeks, and the snow crunched under her boots as she crossed the yard toward the barn. The quiet was a relief after the laughter and teasing, but it didn't last long.

She heard the steady thud of boots behind her.

"You walk fast for someone full of pancakes," Logan drawled.

She didn't turn around. "You lied."

He stopped a few steps behind her, the crunch of his boots halting. "About what?"

"The feed store," she said, spinning to face him. "Why did you say that? My mom's going to want every detail now—where it was, what I was wearing, who said what first—"

His mouth curved, slow and knowing. "You're welcome."

Her brow furrowed. "For what?"

"For saving your ass," he said simply. "You froze up. You looked like you were about to choke on your coffee. Someone had to say something."

"I could've handled it," she said, though even to her own ears, it sounded weak.

"Sure you could've," he said, his voice teasing but low, eyes holding hers. "But I wasn't about to sit there and watch you melt under your mom's questions. Besides…" He stepped closer, his tone softening. "It wasn't that bad of a story."

Avery folded her arms, pretending to be annoyed even as her heart raced. "You could've at least picked something believable."

He tilted his head, the faintest smirk playing on his lips. "You don't think it's believable? You running into me outside a feed store?"

Her throat tightened. "No," she blurted.

He took another step forward. The space between them shrank, heat radiating off him in the chilly morning air. "Because if I remember right, Collins," he murmured, "you did run into me once. Just not outside a feed store."

Her pulse jumped. He was talking about that night in Jackson Hole—a single, fleeting encounter she hadn't been able to forget.

"That was a long time ago," she whispered.

"Yeah," he said, eyes never leaving hers. "And yet, here we are."

For a heartbeat, the only sound was the wind whistling through the barn doors.

Then he reached past her, grabbing a halter from the wall, breaking the tension like he hadn't just set her nerves on fire. "Your brother's out here somewhere, pretending he knows how to saddle a horse. You might wanna save him before he ends up on his ass."

Avery blinked, thrown by the sudden shift. "You're something else."

He looked over his shoulder, a half-smile tugging at his mouth. "You keep saying that, Doc, but you're still here."

She watched him walk toward the stalls, sunlight glinting off the snow-dusted brim of his hat. And for reasons she didn't dare examine, she followed—knowing full well she was in more danger than she'd ever been before.

Not from the storm.
 Not from her family's suspicions.
 But from the way Logan Hunter made pretending feel real.

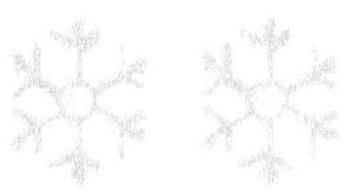

By dusk, the snow had started again—thick, heavy flakes drifting through the fading light, settling like feathers on the rooftops and fences. The ranch seemed quieter now, wrapped in a muffled calm that only winter could bring.

Inside the main cabin, the glow of the fireplace cast a soft light across the room. Avery helped her grandmother set the table, her movements automatic, her mind still back in the barn—in Logan's words, the way his voice had dropped when he said *you're not enough for people who say they love you.*

He'd said it like he knew. Like he'd lived it.

Her grandmother, sharp as ever despite her age, gave her a knowing look. "You've been quiet tonight, sweetheart. Is everything all right?"

Avery forced a small smile. "Just tired. Long day."

"Mm-hmm." Her grandmother's eyes twinkled. "That cowboy of yours seems to know how to keep you on your toes."

"Grandma—" Avery started, cheeks warming, but before she could finish, the door swung open.

Logan stepped in, snow melting off his jacket, boots thudding softly against the floorboards. He paused when he saw her—just a heartbeat of hesitation—but it was enough to make her chest tighten.

"Evening," he said, his voice lower, softer than usual. "Smells good in here."

Her mother smiled from the stove. "Dinner's almost ready. Why don't you sit? You look like you've been through a storm yourself."

"Feels like it," he said, glancing briefly at Avery.

As everyone gathered around the table, laughter and conversation filled the air. Her father asked about the ranch, her brother recounted his disastrous attempt at riding earlier, and her grandmother fussed over the biscuits being too brown. But through it all, Avery felt Logan's gaze on her—steady, unreadable, almost protective.

When she reached for the salt, his hand brushed hers. The touch was brief, accidental maybe, but it sent a current straight through her. He didn't move his hand away immediately.

And for a moment, with her family talking around them, the world felt suspended—just the two of them, caught between the lie they were living and the truth neither dared to name.

After dinner, her family drifted off to their rooms, leaving Avery to tidy the kitchen. Logan lingered by the fire, his profile lit in amber light. She tried to ignore the way her pulse jumped every time he moved.

After she rinsed the last dish, she turned and found him watching her.

"You okay?" he asked quietly.

She hesitated. "You said something earlier. In the barn."

He leaned against the counter, arms crossed, expression unreadable. "I say a lot of things, Collins."

"This one felt different," she whispered. "Like you meant it."

He didn't answer right away. The fire popped, the wind howled softly outside, and for once, he looked… uncertain.

"Maybe I did," he said finally. "I know what it's like to put on a show for people who expect more than you can give. You tire of pretending."

Her breath caught. "You think that's what I'm doing?"

He met her eyes then, gaze dark and steady. "I think it's what we're both doing."

The silence stretched between them—thick, charged, and fragile.

Avery took a small step closer, her voice barely above a whisper. "Maybe pretending isn't so bad… when you're doing it with the right person."

Logan's jaw flexed, and for a heartbeat, it looked like he might close the distance between them. But then he exhaled, slow and controlled, stepping back instead.

"Careful, Doc," he murmured. "You say things like that, and I might start thinking it's real."

Her lips parted, words caught in her throat.

He turned away, tossing another log onto the fire. "Get some rest," he breathed. "Tomorrow's going to be a long day."

She stood there for a moment, heart racing, torn between relief and regret.

Because what she wanted—what they both wanted—they already expressed in every look, every breath, every moment they let linger too long.

And as they headed toward the room, the snow outside thickened, blanketing the ranch once again. The storm might have been quiet this time—but inside, something far more dangerous was stirring.

Chapter 8

Firelight & Flirtation

Avery woke to the pale gray of dawn slipping through the cabin window, soft and cold against her skin. The bed beside her was empty, the sheet cool where Logan had slept before retreating to the couch again—always careful, always keeping that invisible line between them. He was a man who respected boundaries—even when every muscle in his body ached to break them.

She stretched, the soft flannel sheets rustling, and padded barefoot through the cabin. The faint scent of coffee and cedar lingered in the air. When she reached the kitchen window, she froze. Outside, Logan moved through the snow with the effortless grace of someone who belonged to the land. His broad shoulders flexed under a worn brown jacket as he worked, the steam of his breath visible in the chilly morning air.

She smiled. There was something grounding about him—something raw and unpolished that made her chest tighten.

Pulling on her coat, Avery stepped outside. The cold bit her cheeks, but the crisp air felt alive against her skin. Logan turned at the sound of her boots crunching through the frost.

"Morning, beautiful," he called, his voice low and warm, rolling over her like molasses.

Avery flushed. "Morning. Need a hand?"

He chuckled. "Are you volunteering to muck stalls, Doc?"

"If you teach me."

He tipped his hat, eyes glinting. "Careful what you offer."

They worked side by side for a while—Logan feeding the horses, Avery awkwardly trying to copy his rhythm. The animals seemed to like her; one chestnut mare nuzzled against her shoulder as if sensing her gentleness.

When Logan saddled his horse, Avery watched the ease of his movements, the power beneath his calm.

"I was about to check the fence lines," he said. "Storm's coming tonight, best to make sure everything's tight."

"Can I come?" she asked, surprising herself. "I'd like to see the ranch."

He hesitated for a heartbeat, then nodded. "All right. But you ride with me."

She didn't argue.

As Logan helped Avery into the saddle, he smirked. "Hold on tight, Doc. Horses don't care if you have a PhD."

Avery laughed nervously. "I'll try not to fall off your perfect ranch."

"Perfect, huh?" he teased, nudging her with his shoulder. "I guess that makes me your rugged, handsome tour guide."

She rolled her eyes but felt a thrill run through her as he guided the horse. Every brush of his arm, the scent of cedar and leather, and the warmth of his body made her pulse quicken.

They rode through the expanse of snow-dusted pasture, the world quiet except for the creak of saddle leather and the soft rhythm of hooves.

As they passed the chicken coop, a clucking hen darted under their horse. Avery squealed. "Watch it!"

Logan chuckled, an indistinct sound that made her stomach flutter. "See? Even the chickens are trying to distract you."

Logan spoke softly as they continued to ride—about the land, the livestock, the long winters and the stubborn pride it took to survive them. His voice carried both love and loneliness.

Avery admired that—his devotion. She also saw her own obsession with medicine reflected in it.

When they returned to the barn, Avery brushed the mare down while Logan hauled water and hay. Her eyes wandered to a coil of rope hanging on the wall. She absently ran her fingers along the coarse fibers, feeling the texture under her fingertips.

Logan's voice came from behind her, low and edged with heat. "Careful, sweetheart," he drawled. "You play with things like that, you'll give a man the wrong idea."

When she turned, he smirked. "Or the right kind."

Avery froze, a small smirk tugging at her lips despite herself. "Idea?"

He leaned closer, so close she could feel the warmth of his body and the faint scent of cedar and leather. "Like how I'd love to tie you up with it someday."

Her pulse stuttered, heat pooling low in her belly, shocking in its intensity. She couldn't bring herself to turn around—afraid that if she looked at him, she wouldn't be able to breathe.

She tried to sound casual, lifting her eyebrows. "Oh, so the rope isn't just for horses?"

Logan chuckled softly, dark and knowing. "Maybe I'm just pointing out the obvious… or maybe I'm giving you a warning."

She rolled her eyes, though her cheeks warmed. "You're incorrigible."

"And you love it," he whispered, his voice dipping lower, teasing.

Avery's stomach fluttered, caught between irritation and desire. Logan gave her a slow grin before finally stepping back. "Come on," he said, his tone softening. "We've got company tonight. Let's save the 'ropework' for later."

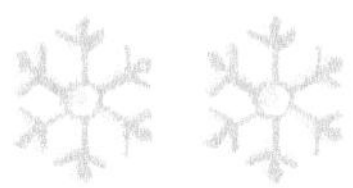

That evening, the ranch was alive with laughter and clinking glasses. Avery's family had come for dinner, brightening the place with a bit of joy. She'd thought, this is nice, her family being normal for once. She'd worried they might notice the act—but Logan was effortlessly charming, answering questions, making her father laugh, wrapping his arm around her shoulders like he'd been doing it all his life.

For a moment, she almost believed it herself.

Then her father spoke, his voice cutting through the cheer.
 "You know, Logan, we should thank you. We never thought Avery would ever get married. Especially with that PCOS thing she's got going on… probably won't have kids with her condition. Good luck with that."

Avery froze, her fork halfway to her mouth.

Her stomach twisted. Her brother added, "She always complains like life isn't hard for everyone."

Her mother sighed, swirling her wine. "She's always been difficult. Never finishes what she starts. I'm shocked she even made it through med school. All she does is complain and sleep in. I'm surprised she even has time to see patients."

Laughter rippled through the table.

It was the sound that finally cracked her. The same laughter she'd grown up hearing every time she dared to speak too loudly, dream too big, or cry too openly.

Avery stared down at her plate, her throat tight. She forced a smile, but her hands trembled. The heat of humiliation crawled up her neck as they kept talking—about her PCOS, her moods, her supposed failures.

Finally, she stood. "Excuse me."

The room went quiet. She turned, fled down the hall, her vision blurring.

Logan watched her go, something dark flickering in his chest. Then he stood—slowly, deliberately—and looked at her family.

The room buzzed with laughter. Logan's jaw flexed once, twice, before he stood—slow, deliberate, like a man readying for a fight.

"That's enough."

Her father blinked. "Excuse me?"

Logan's voice was rough, anger restrained. "You heard me. You don't get to walk into my home and tear down my wife like she's nothing. You don't get to laugh at her pain."

"She's our daughter," her mother protested.

"She's my wife," Logan shot back. "And I'll have no one disrespecting her—especially not her own damn family."

Silence. Then, one by one, they gathered their things and left, muttering about "touchy cowboys" and "overreacting."

Logan didn't care. He was already moving down the hall.

He found Avery curled on the bed, her back to him, shoulders shaking. The sight hit him like a fist.

"Avery," he whispered, sitting beside her. "Baby, look at me."

She didn't. "It's fine," she whispered. "I'm used to it. They're right, you know. I'm a burden. You don't have to keep this up. I can go."

He swore under his breath. "Jesus, no."

She finally turned, eyes red and wet. "Logan—"

He cupped her face gently. "You are *not* a burden. You're the strongest damn woman I've ever met.

They can't see it, but I do. And I swear to you, Avery Collins—Hunter—whatever name you want to claim, you deserve everything good in this world."

Her breath hitched. He pulled her against him, pressing a kiss to her forehead, his thumb brushing away her tears.

And for the first time since they'd started pretending, Avery didn't resist. She let herself melt into his warmth, into the safety of his arms.

Logan held her until her shaking stopped. When they finally lay down, his arm draped over her waist, the line between real and fake blurred completely.

Outside, the snow fell softly and endlessly, burying the world in silence. Inside, beneath the hush of the storm, something inside Avery finally thawed—slow, fragile, and real.

Chapter 9

Cowboy Smirk, Racing Pulse

Avery stepped onto the porch, crisp winter air biting at her cheeks. The ranch stretched before her—quiet, white, breathtaking. Logan leaned against the railing, hat tilted low, one boot propped on the post. That smirk—the one that always stole her breath—curved slowly and deliberately.

"Morning, beautiful," he drawled. "Careful. Frost like this'll steal your breath… if a cowboy doesn't beat it to it."

Avery rolled her eyes, pulse already racing. "I think I can handle the cold. And you."

"Mmh." His gaze swept her face with infuriating confidence. "We'll see."

Before she could fire back, snow crunched along the path. Her parents' friends—Karen and David Whitman, and Jake Benson—approached, bundled in scarves and curiosity.

Avery's stomach tightened. She knew those looks: the same old silent judgments wrapped behind polite holiday smiles.

Logan noticed instantly. His hand brushed her arm—steadying, grounding.

"You good?" he murmured.

She nodded, even though she wasn't.

Inside the cabin, warmth and conversation swelled. Logan slipped seamlessly into host mode—greeting the guests, shaking hands, guiding Avery into the fold like he'd been doing it forever. His arm draped lazily across her shoulders, the kind of casual affection that made her heart stutter.

Karen grinned. "So, Logan—must be a handful keeping up with a doctor."

Logan's gaze flicked down to Avery. "She keeps me on my toes. I wouldn't have it any other way."

Her chest tightened at the sincerity under the tease.

Jake snorted. "Didn't think Avery would ever settle down. She's always been… intense. Even with the body issues, she's tough—but moody."

Avery stiffened, embarrassment prickling hot.

Logan's smile vanished.

"Jake," he said quietly. Dangerously. "Watch your mouth. Not in my house and definitely not about my wife."

The room froze. Even the fire seemed to still.

Avery blinked, stunned. No one had ever defended her like that—not without making her feel small.

Jake lifted his hands in surrender. "Alright, alright."

Logan kept staring until the man looked away.

When the tension finally broke, Logan resumed his charm like nothing happened. Everyone laughed again—everyone but Avery, who was still reeling from the way his protectiveness had punched straight into her chest.

Later, as she moved through the room passing cocoa out, Karen drifted toward Logan, touching his arm, and clearly flirting with him, far too easily. Avery watched, jaw tightening.

Logan returned to her side moments later, handing her a mug.

"You okay?" he asked, amusement flickering in his eyes.

"Fine," she muttered.

"Mmh." He leaned in, voice low. "You were glaring holes through her."

"I was not."

"You were jealous, Doc."

Avery scoffed. "I was protecting our cover."

He stepped closer, cedar and warmth wrapping around her like a pull she couldn't escape. "That's why you looked ready to climb across the counter when she touched me?"

She swallowed. "She was all over you."

"And I didn't care," he said softly. "Not once."

Her heartbeat stumbled.

When the guests finally left and the cabin quieted, Avery gathered dishes, trying to steady her emotions. Logan joined her at the sink, sleeves rolled up, forearms flexing as he rinsed mugs. Every movement was precise, unhurried.

"Thanks for helping," she said.

He glanced over his shoulder, lips curving. "Thanks for the jealousy. Kind of enjoyed it."

"Don't push your luck."

"Not pushing," he murmured. "Just saying that if you wanted me to yourself, all you had to do was ask."

Her breath caught. "Logan—"

He stepped closer, towel forgotten. "Looked real to me tonight," he said quietly. "Every time you touch me. Every time I touched you. Pretend or not."

Avery's heart hammered.

She turned away first. "We should finish cleaning."

"Mmh." His voice dropped, rough. "Before I decide the kitchen's too small for all this… tension."

When the last dish was stacked, she leaned back on the counter, exhausted and restless all at once.

Logan stood across from her, arms crossed, eyes dark and unreadable.

"You surprised me tonight," he said.

"How?"

"You fought for me." His voice softened. "Didn't know you had that in you."

She lifted her chin. "Maybe I just don't like sharing."

A slow, dangerous smile spread across his face. "Good. Because for the record? I wasn't thinking about Karen. Not even for a second."

Her breath hitched.

"Goodnight, Doc," he murmured, stepping past her—close enough that his arm brushed hers. "Before I forget we're supposed to be pretending."

He walked out, leaving Avery alone in the quiet kitchen, heart racing, hands trembling, and painfully aware that pretending was becoming impossible.

Outside, snow blanketed the ranch—but the real storm was in her chest.

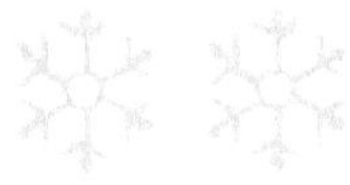

Logan's POV

Logan hadn't meant to snap at her father's friend.

Hell, he hadn't meant to do half the things he'd done tonight.

But the second he heard those words come out of the man's mouth—words meant to cut her down, even wrapped in a joke—something inside him burned hot and fast. He'd spent his whole life around rough talk, men running their mouths, people throwing jabs. But hearing someone talk that way about Avery?

Yeah. No.

Not in his house.

As he rinsed the last mug at the sink, he kept catching glimpses of her—Avery, pretending she wasn't rattled, pretending she wasn't jealous, pretending she didn't feel anything at all.

She was terrible at pretending.

He hadn't expected that. He hadn't expected any of this.

The way she'd stepped closer to him earlier.

The way she'd stiffened when Karen pressed her hand to his arm.

The way her voice had gone quiet when he defended her—shock and something else flashing in her eyes.

He'd stood up for women before. Family. Friends. But this… this had felt different.

He'd meant every damn word.

When the kitchen finally quieted and Avery leaned against the counter, cheeks flushed from anger and something warmer, Logan felt that old familiar pull in his chest—the one he tried real hard to ignore.

Dangerous.

Unwanted.

Impossible to shake.

God, she had no idea the effect she had on him.

Avery Collins—brilliant, stubborn, impossible, gorgeous Avery—looked at him like he was someone worth being jealous over. Someone worth choosing. Someone who mattered.

And that scared the hell out of him.

He watched her from the doorway now, the firelight touching the edges of her hair, catching in her eyes. She looked soft in that light. Vulnerable. Real.

Too real.

She doesn't know what she's doing, he told himself.

She doesn't know what she's stirring up.

But he knew.

Tanisha Pollard

He felt every bit of it.

Every time she blushed.

Every time she glared at him.

Every time she stepped close, only to pretend she didn't mean it.

She was getting under his skin in ways he didn't have a name for.

When he told her goodnight—when he turned and left the room—it wasn't because he wanted space.

It was because if he stayed one second longer, he was going to do something he couldn't take back.

Something that would blur every line they'd drawn.

He closed his bedroom door and leaned his back against it, exhaling hard.

"Get a grip, Hunter," he muttered into the dark.

But even as he said it, he knew the truth.

He was already in trouble.

And Avery Collins…

She had no idea how close he was to falling.

Chapter 10

Dangerous Desire

Avery stretched as pale sunlight filtered through the cabin windows, painting the wooden walls in soft gold. The house was still—almost *too* still. Her family had taken advantage of the cloudless morning to visit a nearby ski resort, leaving her and Logan alone on the ranch.
The thought of it being just them made her chest flutter in ways she wasn't ready to name.

From the kitchen window, she spotted him outside. Logan moved through the snow with the same quiet confidence—feeding the horses, checking the fences, his breath a faint cloud in the cold air. The worn brown jacket hugged his broad shoulders, the sure rhythm of movement making her pulse stutter.

Pulling on her coat, Avery stepped outside. The cold bit her cheeks, crisp and clean. Logan turned at the sound of her boots crunching through the snow, a slow grin curving his mouth.

"Morning, beautiful," he drawled, voice warm enough to melt frost.

"Morning," she said, tucking a strand of hair behind her ear. "Need a hand with the horses?"

He tipped his hat, eyes glinting. "You sure you can handle it, Doc?"

"I can handle it… plus you showed me once already," she shot back, teasing despite the nervous flutter in her chest.

Logan chuckled, that low, lazy sound that did dangerous things to her heartbeat. "Careful what you offer, Avery. I've been known to make a girl sweat."

She laughed softly, shaking her head as they headed for the barn. Inside, the smell of hay and cedar wrapped around her, warm and earthy. They fell into a peaceful rhythm—feeding, brushing, checking stalls. Avery's hands lingered on the chestnut mare's glossy coat, the horse leaning into her gentle touch.

"You've got a way with them," Logan said, voice dropping to that dark, teasing tone. "Almost makes me wonder what else you could handle if I put you in… a different kind of harness."

Avery froze mid-stroke, breath catching. "Harness? What does that mean?"

He leaned against the post, eyes steady on hers, a half-smile playing at his lips. "Maybe I just mean guiding you. Keeping you steady. Showing you how to *trust* someone else to take control."

Her pulse jumped. She focused on the horse again, pretending she wasn't trembling.

Logan chuckled under his breath, rich and knowing. "All right, Doc. You can keep focusing on the horse. Just know you're not fooling me—your blush gives you away every time."

By midday, they'd made a slow loop of the property. Avery rode behind him, her hands resting lightly on his waist as the horse moved through drifts of powdery snow. Each sway of his body drew her closer; each breath seemed to sync with his.

"You know," Logan said over his shoulder, voice lazy, "every time you get this close, I forget what I'm supposed to be doing."

"Pretty sure it's fixing fences," she managed, her voice softer than she intended.

He laughed, the sound low and rough. "Right. Fences. Gotta keep things contained."

But nothing in the air between them felt contained.

By the time they returned to the barn, the sun had dipped, staining the snow in shades of rose and amber. Avery brushed down the mare while Logan stacked hay, his shirt clinging to the muscles across his back. The silence between them hummed and charged.

Inside, the cabin welcomed them with warmth and quiet. Avery poured herself a mug of cocoa, but her thoughts lingered on Logan—the way he moved, the way his teasing left her breathless.

When he leaned in the doorway, arms folded, watching her with that dark, unreadable gaze, the air seemed to shift again.

"Dangerous," he murmured. "How much you affect me without even trying."

Her breath caught. "You shouldn't say things like that."

He took a slow step closer. "Why not? It's the truth."

The space between them disappeared. Avery could feel his heat, smell the faint cedar on his skin. The moment stretched, soft and electric.

Then Logan exhaled, stepping back just enough to give her room to breathe. "You make it really hard to keep my promises, Doc."

Avery's heart thudded. "What promises?"

He smiled, slow and wistfully. "The ones that keep me from doing something we can't take back."

Outside, the snow fell again, blanketing the world in silence. Inside, the quiet between them said everything neither dared to admit.

And somewhere deep down, Avery knew—storms weren't the only things impossible to control.

Chapter 11

Snowed–In Temptation

The snow started before dinner—soft flakes tumbling through the air like ash from a dying fire. By the time they finished in the barn, the wind had turned wild, swallowing the horizon in a blur of white.

"Looks like we're not going anywhere," Logan said, latching the barn door. His voice was a low rumble under the wind, his hair dusted with snow, his breath warm in the cold.

Avery rubbed her gloved hands together. "You're telling me we're stuck here?"

He gave her that half-smile that always undid her. "Unless you've got wings I don't know about, sweetheart, we're snowed in."

Something about the way he said *sweetheart* made her pulse skip.

Inside the cabin, the fire snapped to life, chasing shadows from the corners. The heat crawled across the floorboards, across her skin. Logan hung his jacket by the door and crouched by the hearth, the muscles in his back shifting beneath his shirt as he fed the flames.

"Remind me to thank the weatherman later," he said.

Avery shot him a look over her shoulder. "For trapping us on a mountain of snow?"

"For giving me an excuse to stay right here." He straightened, nodding toward the window. "No signal. No traffic. There's no one to knock on that door. Just us."

She tried for sarcasm, but it came out breathy. "How terrifying."

His grin curved slowly. "Don't worry. I bite only when invited."

Her laugh trembled. "You're impossible."

"And yet," he said softly, "you haven't told me to leave you alone."

They set up camp in the living room—two mugs of cocoa, an old deck of cards, and the storm murmuring like a heartbeat outside. After a few hands of gin rummy and two accusations of cheating, Avery leaned back against the couch, smiling despite herself.

"Okay, new rule," she said. "Every time you win, you tell me something real. No charming cowboy lines."

He tapped the cards against his palm. "Define *real*."

"Something you wouldn't tell just anyone."

His eyes flicked to the fire. "All right." He set the cards down, voice lowering. "When I was a kid, I used to sneak into the stables at night. Not to ride—just to listen. Horses breathe differently when the world's quiet. You can hear them dream."

Avery blinked. "That's… unexpectedly poetic."

He smirked. "Don't tell anyone. It'd ruin my reputation."

Her heart squeezed. "Okay. My turn. I used to think I'd leave my hometown the second I graduated. Go somewhere no one knows me or my family or my body's broken clock."
 Her voice cracked, soft. "Now I'm not sure I'd know how to start over."

The room went still. Logan's expression softened, stripped of its usual mischief.
 "You're not broken, Avery."

She gave a small, shaky smile. "Tell that to my ovaries."

He reached across the table and brushed his fingers over hers—just a whisper of touch, but it burned through her. "If they were mine, I'd say they're stubborn. Not broken."

Her breath caught. "You always know what to say, don't you?"

"Only when I mean it."

They talked until the cocoa went cold—about her clinic plans, the way Wyoming smelled before a storm, the first time he'd lost a rodeo and how it gutted him. With every story, every laugh, the air between them grew heavier—closer.

At some point, she leaned her head on his shoulder. It felt too natural, like her body had been waiting for this shape all along.

"Do you ever tire of being brave?" she asked softly.

He tilted his head toward hers, breath warm against her hair. "Every damn day."

The confession lingered, fragile and unguarded.

Avery turned, eyes catching firelight. "Me too."

Outside, the wind screamed. Inside, the world slowed.

Logan pulled the blanket from the couch and draped it around them both. "Come here," he murmured, voice roughened with something that made her whole body hum.

She shifted closer until her knee brushed his thigh. His warmth seeped into her, steady and consuming. For a long while, they said nothing—just listened to the storm claw at the windows, their breathing quietly syncing.

Then his hand found hers again, tracing lazy, deliberate circles over her skin.

"Are we still playing that truth game?" he asked.

"Maybe," she whispered.

"Then here's mine." His thumb stilled. "I can't tell where pretending ends anymore."

Her heart stumbled. "Maybe it already did."

He leaned in, stopping just shy of her lips. "Tell me to stop."

She didn't.

The kiss was soft at first, cautious, almost reverent. Then deeper—like exhaling after holding her breath for too long. When he pulled back, his forehead rested against hers, both of them suspended in the quiet.

"This isn't pretend anymore, is it?" he whispered.

She shook her head. "No. It's not."

The fire burned low, painting them in gold. Outside, the storm swallowed the world whole.

They stayed wrapped in the blanket, sharing the quiet, the warmth, the fragile truth neither of them could take back.

Avery had thought the danger was being trapped by the storm.
 But as Logan's thumb traced slow, endless circles against her palm, she realized the real danger was him — the way he looked at her like she wasn't something to fix, but someone he'd already chosen.

Logan shifted beside her, the movement slow and deliberate before he gently slipped his hand from hers. "Stay warm," he murmured, his voice a low promise as he stood. Avery watched him cross the room, broad shoulders silhouetted in the glow as he stoked the dying fire and added another log to the hearth. Sparks flared, briefly painting his features in molten gold. When he turned back to her, brushing the soot from his hands, there was something softened—and undeniably intent—in his eyes. He came back to her like gravity itself pulled him there.

The storm softened into a quiet whisper against the windows, but inside the cabin the air felt anything but calm. The fire sank into glowing embers, shadows flickering gently across Logan's face as he watched the flames settle. Avery wrapped the blanket tighter around her shoulders, trying—and failing—to steady her breathing.

He hadn't moved far from her, just close enough that she could feel the warmth of him even from across the room. The kind of warmth that seeped into her bones, settling deep and dangerously.

Logan lifted his gaze, eyes catching hers with that slow, careful intensity that always undid her.

"Come here," he murmured, voice low and thick with something she didn't trust herself to name.

She hesitated only a second before he shifted, opening the blanket—an invitation she felt all the way to her toes. Avery crossed the small distance, pulse fluttering like a live wire. The second she sat beside him, Logan pulled the blanket around both of them. His thigh pressed against hers, solid and warm, and the heat rushed up her body so fast she had to bite back a breath.

He didn't touch her at first.

But his presence was a touch all on its own.

Avery leaned into him slowly, testing the moment. Logan's arm slid behind her, hooking loosely around her waist—not pulling, not demanding, just quietly claiming the space between them. Her head found his shoulder before she could second-guess it. The movement felt instinctive. Right. Too right.

His fingers brushed her hip, light as a whisper.

Her breath hitched.

The night flashed in her mind—the laughter, the way he'd looked at her, the raw honesty neither of them had planned… and the kiss. God, the kiss. Soft but consuming. Careful but devastating. She still felt it everywhere.

"About tonight," she whispered, not lifting her head.

Logan's thumb stroked once along her waist, slow enough to melt her. "We don't have to talk about it," he murmured, voice thick. "Not tonight."

"But the kiss…"

She didn't finish.

"Avery." His voice shifted—rougher, closer. She felt him turn toward her. "That wasn't pretend. Not for a second."

Heat curled low in her stomach. The truth in his voice, the quiet hunger beneath it, made her whole body feel weightless.

She tilted her head, looking up at him. "I don't regret it."

His jaw flexed, eyes darkening. "Good," he rasped. "Because if you did… I might've done something stupid like apologize."

Her breath caught on a soft laugh. "You're not going to, are you?"

His hand tightened on her waist, just enough to pull her a fraction closer.

"Not unless you tell me you want me to."

Her heart thundered. "I don't."

Something shifted in him—subtle but unmistakable. His gaze dropped to her mouth for a fleeting second, enough to steal the oxygen from her lungs.

Then he exhaled slowly and leaned back, pulling her fully into his side beneath the blanket.

"You should rest," he murmured against her hair.

His voice had gone too soft—too intimate.

Avery curled into him, her knees drawn up, his arm firm and warm around her. The storm outside faded completely, leaving only the sound of their breaths aligning, the quiet crackle of cooling embers, and the steady beat of his heart under her cheek.

She hadn't meant to let her eyes close.

Hadn't meant to let her guard slip this far.

But Logan was warm.

He was steady.

He was holding her like she belonged there.

And little by little, exhaustion pulled her under.

Right before sleep claimed her, one last thought flickered through her mind—terrifying and beautiful all at once:

She wasn't afraid of the storm anymore.

She was afraid of how safe he made her feel.

Afraid of what tomorrow would bring.

Afraid that one kiss had already changed everything.

Logan's hand smoothed along her arm, slow and protective. His breath rested against her hair as he whispered something she didn't hear fully—her name, maybe, or just a quiet promise he didn't mean to say aloud.

They drifted into sleep together on the couch, wrapped in one blanket, wrapped in something neither of them could pretend away anymore.

Chapter 12

First Surrender

By morning, the storm had eased, leaving the world blanketed in stillness. Snow shimmered across the ranch like glass, untouched and glittering under a pale sun. The cabin was quiet except for the soft crackle of the fireplace and the rhythmic scrape of Logan's boots across the floor.

Avery stirred on the couch, the blanket slipping from her shoulders. For a moment, she wasn't sure what woke her—until she heard the faint hum of Logan's voice.
 He was in the kitchen, humming low and off-key, flipping pancakes in a cast-iron pan.

"You're up early," she murmured, her voice still thick with sleep.

He turned, grinning. "Cowboys don't sleep in, but I figured I'd make breakfast before you sprint to that laptop and drown yourself in patient charts."

Avery smiled, tugging the blanket tighter around her shoulders. "You cooked?"

"I cook all the time." He handed her a plate, his fingers brushing hers—deliberate, light, dangerous. "Plus, I'd say surviving the night with me qualifies as a deserving breakfast."

She rolled her eyes but took a bite, anyway. "It's actually… good."

He leaned against the counter, mug in hand. "You sound surprised."

"I'm just wondering if there's anything you can't do."

"Oh, plenty," he said with a smirk. "But I'm great at pretending I can."

Their laughter filled the room, warm and unguarded. For the first time since she arrived, Avery felt something shift—a softness replacing the guarded tension.

They spent the morning moving through quiet chores. She followed him to the barn, boots crunching through the snow, helping him brush the horses and refill the troughs. When one foal nuzzled into her coat, she giggled, the sound bright and pure.

Logan watched her, leaning against a post, a faint smile tugging at his lips.
 "You belong here more than you think, Doc."

She looked over her shoulder. "You think so?"

He nodded slowly. "You're not afraid of the work. Or the quiet. Most people run from both."

She met his gaze, steady and unflinching. "Maybe I had been running too long already."

Something in his expression softened, like he understood more than he'd ever admit.

By midday, the sun disappeared behind thick clouds again, and the temperature dropped. They worked side by side until the wind picked up, driving them back toward the cabin. Avery's cheeks were pink from the cold, her hair loose around her face. Logan reached out without thinking, brushing a snowflake from her temple.

"You've got frost on your lashes," he murmured.

Her breath caught. "You could've just told me."

"I like the view better up close."

She didn't move. Didn't breathe. The silence stretched until she finally stepped back, her heart pounding in her chest.

"Come on," she whispered. "We'll freeze if we stay out here."

Inside, the cabin filled again with firelight and the faint scent of pine. Logan stoked the flames while Avery brewed tea, both pretending not to notice how quiet it had become between them—how charged.

By evening, the world outside had vanished into white again. The storm had returned, fierce and unrelenting, trapping them together for another night.

Avery sat on the rug near the hearth, pulling the blanket around herself, the same one they'd shared the night before. Logan joined her, sitting close enough that the fabric brushed his leg.

"Déjà vu," he murmured, pouring them each a mug of tea. "The only difference is, last night we were still pretending not to want this."

She smiled faintly. "And tonight?"

"Tonight," he said, his voice low and rough, "I'm not pretending anymore."

Her heart thudded painfully in her chest. "And if I'm still figuring out what I want?"

"Then I'll wait." His eyes softened. "But I need you to know I'm done hiding how I feel."

The honesty in his tone hit her like a blow. For all his teasing, his confidence, this was raw. Real.

Avery looked at him for a long moment—then set her mug down.
 "I don't want you to wait."

Logan's breath hitched. "Avery…"

She reached for him, her hand trembling slightly as she brushed a strand of hair from his face. "You said last night this wasn't pretend anymore. You were right."

He didn't speak, just searched her face as if to make sure she meant it. Then he leaned forward, slowly enough that she could stop him.

She didn't.

Their lips met—soft, questioning at first, then deepening until the space between them disappeared entirely. Every kiss carried everything they hadn't said: the fear, the longing, the fragile trust that bound them tighter with each breath.

Logan pulled back just enough to search her face, his voice a low rasp. "You have no idea what you do to me."

Avery's breath hitched, her pulse racing. "You think you're the only one losing control here?"

A rough laugh escaped him, more like a groan. "Then we're both in trouble."

She smiled, barely. "Guess it's too late to stop now."

"Way too late," he murmured, brushing his thumb across her lower lip before kissing her again—deeper this time, hungrier.

Her hands fisted in his shirt, pulling him closer until there was no space left to think, only feel. His breath mingled with hers, warm and unsteady.

Between kisses, she whispered, "You keep looking at me like that…"

"Like what?" he asked, voice gravelly.

"Like you're about to ruin me."

His lips curved against hers, dangerous and soft all at once. "Sweetheart, I think that ship's already sailed."

Her breath caught, the world narrowing to the rough scrape of his stubble against her skin and the steady thud of his heart beneath her palm. Logan's hand slid up her back, steady but reverent, like he was memorizing every inch of her.

"Avery," he whispered against her jaw, her name a quiet confession.

She tilted her head back, eyes fluttering shut. "Say it again."

He did—so softly it almost broke her. "Avery."

Something inside her unraveled at the sound. All the walls she'd built, all the careful lines she'd drawn, dissolved beneath the heat of his touch.

Her fingers found his collar, tugging him closer. "You make it impossible to think straight," she breathed.

Logan gave a low chuckle, his forehead resting against hers. "Good. I'm tired of pretending I'm not falling for you."

Her heart stumbled. "Then don't pretend," she whispered.

That was all it took. His mouth found hers again—deeper, slower, like a promise he meant to keep. The wind howled outside, but inside the cabin, everything was warm and breathless. The fire popped in the hearth, casting flickers of gold across his skin as their shadows moved closer, merging in the dim light.

The cocoa sat forgotten on the counter.

And as the storm raged on outside, the real one—raw and consuming—rose quietly between them.

His thumb traced the corner of her mouth, lingering there like he couldn't quite believe she was real.

"Tell me to stop," he murmured, his voice rough and unsteady.

Avery met his gaze—steady, breathless, sure. "Don't you dare."

That was all it took. The restraint in his eyes shattered, replaced by a hunger that made her pulse stutter. His lips crashed into hers again, no hesitation this time—just heat and need and everything they'd both been trying so hard to ignore.

Her hands found his shoulders, strong and solid beneath her fingers. He caught her waist, pulling her closer until there wasn't an inch of space left between them. The world outside ceased to exist—no storm, no doubts, no pretending. Just him. Just her.

Somewhere in the background, the fire crackled, throwing sparks against the glass.

"Logan…" Her voice trembled against his lips.

He smiled, slow and sinfully. "Yeah, Doc?"

She swallowed hard, her fingers curling in his shirt. "Don't stop."

He didn't.

Logan's kiss deepened, slow and unhurried, like he wanted to memorize every sound she made. His hands slid down her sides, tracing the curve of her waist until they found her hips. The firelight painted his skin in gold; the room shrank to the rhythm of their breaths.

Avery's back met the edge of the table, but she barely noticed. His touch was everywhere—gentle, certain, reverent. When he finally pulled away, their foreheads still touching, he whispered against her lips, "Upstairs."

Her pulse fluttered, wild and reckless.

"Logan…"

"Tell me no," he whispered, even though his voice betrayed him—hoarse, rough, needing.

She didn't. She reached only for his hand, fingers trembling as they laced with his.

The world outside was a blur of snow and wind, but inside, everything burned steadily and bright.

He led her through the dim hallway; the firelight chasing their shadows along the walls. Neither spoke; they didn't have to. Every step, every breath was a silent agreement of what came next.

By the time they reached the bedroom door, Avery turned to him, her eyes dark with want. "Are you sure about this?" she asked, voice barely a whisper.

Logan brushed a strand of hair from her face, his thumb tracing her jaw. "I've never been more sure of anything in my life."

Her breath caught. "Then don't make me wait."

He smiled, that slow, dangerous curve she was craving. "I wouldn't dream of it."

The door clicked shut behind them, sealing out the world.

Avery's back pressed lightly against the wood as Logan stopped in front of her—close enough that she could feel the warmth radiating from his body, the steady rise and fall of his chest. For a heartbeat, neither of them moved. The air between them pulsed with unspoken need.

He lifted a hand, brushing his thumb along her bottom lip as if he were committing it to memory. "You sure you want this?" he asked quietly, though his voice was already thick with want.

She nodded, her breath trembling. "I've wanted this longer than I should've."

That was all it took.

Logan leaned in, his mouth finding hers again, hungrier this time—no hesitation, no pretending. His kiss was rough silk, demanding and tender all at once. Avery melted into him, her fingers clutching the fabric of his shirt, desperate to feel more.

When he deepened the kiss, she gasped softly, and he caught the sound like a secret, his hand sliding to the back of her neck. Everything between them turned molten—every touch, every breath pulling them further past the point of return.

He broke the kiss just long enough to whisper against her skin, "Tell me where you want me, Doc."

Her answer was a breathless laugh, half-plea, half-confession. "Anywhere you'll have me."

Logan lifted her in his arms and pressed her against the door. Avery gasped, somewhere in the back of her mind she couldn't believe he could actually lift her considering everyone in her life said she was way too heavy but she had to let that thought go because what his mouth was doing to her was chasing away all traces of shame right now.

He slowly trailed kisses down her neck. Unable to wait anymore, he ripped her shirt straight down the middle as he trailed soft and tender kisses over her breasts. He stopped to admire her body.

He looked her in the eye.

"Are you sure you want this?" he asked, for the last time, voice rough and steady all at once.
 "Yes," she breathed. "I've never been sure of anything."

His jaw flexed as if he were holding back every ounce of control.

"Then you're mine tonight, Doc."

The words weren't a command—they were a promise.

Avery's pulse fluttered as his hand drifted down her arm, slow and deliberate, until his fingers brushed hers.

"Trust me?" he murmured.
 "Always."

He smiled—small, dark, and devastating.

"Good. Because I plan to make sure you remember this."

The firelight caught in his eyes as he leaned close, lips grazing her ear.

"If I go too far—"
 "You won't," she cut in softly. "I trust you, Logan."

Something broke in his expression then—a flicker of emotion deeper than desire.

"You're gonna ruin me, Doc," he rasped.

Her breath shuddered, the warmth between them building until it was almost unbearable.

His gaze held hers, steady and searching, as if asking one more time if she was sure.

Every inch of space between them hummed with anticipation, heavy and electric.

He laid her on the bed and undressed her.

Avery closed her eyes as he undressed her.

 "Don't close your eyes," he whispered. "I want you to see everything."

So she didn't.

As Logan admired her nakedness, she felt self-conscious of her body, the curves she didn't like or her thighs that were too big, but when he looked at her, she felt beautiful.

He kissed her again, but deeper this time, like the restraint he was holding onto had finally snapped. He sucked on her neck, leaving little lovebites there. Trailing down to her full breasts, he cupped one and toyed with her nipple as he sucked the other into his mouth, causing her back to arch involuntarily.

"Logan," she gasped.

"Don't move, Avery," he hoarsely replied.

He moved to the other nipple, causing her to moan loudly.

"Logan, please, I need you," she begged.

He continued his delicious torture, trailing wet kisses down her stomach, until he reached her center.

He ran his nose up the inside of her thigh, inhaling deeply and allowing her scent to fill him until his mouth watered to taste her.

"Mmm, darlin', you smell so fucking good."

Avery moaned softly, silently begging him to continue.

"Logan, please," she begged.

He wasted no time as he flicked the tip of his tongue along her wet, dripping center.

Avery lifted her hips to meet his mouth.

"Avery, don't move," he commanded. But she didn't listen; her loud moans filled the room.

Logan groaned as her taste flooded him. How could anyone ever resist her?

"Darlin', you taste so fucking sweet, you might be my new favorite dessert."

Logan wrapped his arms around her thighs, holding her wide open for him. As he licked and sucked, her moans grew louder, as if she was urging him on.

"Logan." His name fell from her lips on a satisfied moan. But Logan gave her no mercy as he continued his torture, sucking her clit until she came shaking violently in his arms, begging him to give her release.

He stood watching her as he stripped off his clothes slowly, as she watched his every movement.

She gaped as she saw his length, wondering how sore she was going to be the next day.

Logan crawled over her, gazing into her eyes with a silent promise never to leave. He kissed her as he slowly slid into her, warming her body up to his full length. For her and his benefit, he thrust into her slowly. He was holding back from destroying her.

Avery gasped. "Logan," she began, but before she could finish, he slammed his full length into her as he swallowed her loud moans.

He began thrusting into her without holding back. "Fuck Avery, you're so goddamn tight."

Avery came undone beneath him as he fucked her relentlessly.

Logan pulled out of her and flipped her over. He rubbed the tip of his cock up and down her slit. Logan slammed into her so hard that Avery fell forward. He pulled her back to him and slapped her ass hard. Avery groaned at the sensation she felt. Logan thrust into her repeatedly. She fucked him back as she met his every thrust. Logan groaned as he felt his balls tightening. He knew he was about to cum.

He reached around their bodies, and when he found her clit, he pinched it, sending her screaming. Her orgasm hit her so hard he felt it as her walls squeezed him so tightly he couldn't hold back anymore and came with her.

Logan took a moment to recover before he got up and went to the bathroom to grab a warm washcloth to clean her up.

He returned to the bed and softly cleaned her, although she hissed softly at the sudden tenderness.

They lay together cuddled up in bed. Avery lay curled against Logan's chest as snow and silence muffled the world outside. His hand traced slow, lazy patterns down her arm, his touch tender where his strength had once been fierce.

Neither spoke for a long time.

Then, in the storm's hush, he whispered, "Are you okay?"

Avery smiled against his skin. "I've never been better."

He kissed the top of her head, his voice rough. "Good, because I couldn't live with myself if you regretted this."

"I don't," she murmured, drifting closer, her body fitting against his like they were made to find each other in the dark.

Outside, the storm howled. Inside, Avery realized that surrender didn't always mean weakness—sometimes it was the bravest thing a heart could do.

Chapter 13

Morning After Sparks

Avery woke to the soft crackle of the dying fire and the steady rhythm of Logan's breathing at her back. For one disoriented second, she didn't know where she was—only that the warmth pressed against her felt… safe.

Then it all rushed back.

The kiss.

The surrender.

The way he'd held her like she was something he'd been afraid to touch and terrified to lose.

Logan's arm was draped across her waist, heavy and sure. His breath brushed her neck, warm enough to make her pulse quicken.

He murmured something in his sleep—something that sounded dangerously like mine.

Her stomach flipped.

Sunlight spilled through the frosted window, turning the untouched snowdrifts gold. The world was still but her heart was anything but.

"Your thoughts are showing, Doc," Logan rasped behind her.

She stiffened. "You were supposed to still be asleep."

"I was," he murmured, shifting so his chest pressed more firmly to her back. "But then you started squirming. Figured either you're uncomfortable… or trying to sneak out before breakfast."

"I wasn't sneaking."

She turned, and the sight of him—hair tousled, jaw shadowed, sheets low on his hips—hit her like a blow. He looked wrecked from sleep and better than any man had the right to.

His lazy grin didn't help. "Good. 'Cause I was planning to feed you before I let you go anywhere."

"Feed me?" she echoed.

"Have you ever had ranch-style pancakes?"

Avery narrowed her eyes. "Is that a real thing?"

"Absolutely." He stretched, muscles rippling. "Made them up myself."

"You mean you burn them."

"Only the first one." His grin widened. "Come on. Before I decide to keep you in bed instead."

Her cheeks warmed. She followed him into the kitchen, wrapping herself in a blanket. He moved around the stove like he owned the space—barefoot, easy, domestic in a way that made her chest ache.

When he caught her staring, he smirked.

"Stare at me like that and I'll burn the whole cabin down."

"You're impossible."

"Yeah," he said gently. "But you like me that way."

She didn't deny it.

Breakfast came out slightly lopsided but warm and sweet, the cabin filling with the scent of butter and syrup. They sat across from each other, the silence soft, not strained.

It should've felt awkward. It didn't.

If anything, the quiet felt... intimate.

"So what's the plan today?" Logan asked, sipping his coffee. "Or am I keepin' you hostage another day?"

"I need to check in with the women's clinic," she said. "They rely on me for PCOS outreach—treatment plans, support, the usual."

His brows lifted. "That's the part of your life I don't get to see much."

She blinked, surprised. "You… want to see it?"

"I want to see you," he said simply. "All of you."

Her breath caught.

He drove her into town, handling the icy roads like second nature. At the clinic, he followed her through the halls, watching her work with that quiet, focused intensity she was beginning to recognize as affection.

When a nurse called out, "Dr. Avery! The cowboy finally came to town?" she nearly tripped over her clipboard.

Logan tipped his hat. "Guess my reputation's spread."

"Guess so," she muttered, cheeks hot.

By noon, every woman over fifty adored him. Avery wasn't sure whether to kiss him again or shove him back into the truck.

"You're insufferable," she told him as they drove home.

"How so?"

"You make everyone fall for you."

He shot her a slow look. "Everyone?"

She rolled her eyes. "Most people."

"Mmh." His smirk deepened. "You included?"

"Don't push your luck, cowboy."

But the smile tugging at her lips gave her away.

That evening, they drifted back to the barn—their place of blurred lines and breathless tension. Golden light spilled through the rafters, dust motes drifting like slow sparks.

Logan leaned against a stall post, arms folded. "You looked good today."

"Good?"

He stepped closer. "Confident. Alive. Like you fit in both worlds—mine and yours."

Her chest tightened. "And where do I fit with you?"

He tucked a strand of hair behind her ear. "Still figuring that out."

The air between them shifted, warm and fragile.

"You're shaking," he murmured, fingertips brushing her wrist.

"It's cold," she whispered.

"No." His eyes held hers. "It's not."

She didn't move. Neither did he. The barn seemed to hold its breath.

"Logan…"

"Do you want me to stop?"

"No, I don't want you to."

He kissed her—slow and certain—deepening the moment she leaned into him. This wasn't the desperate storm-driven heat of before. This was deliberate. Tender. A promise forming in the quiet.

When he pulled back, his forehead rested against hers.

"You drive me crazy, Doc."

"Good," she said, breathless. "You deserve it."

He laughed softly, kissing her again, the sound rumbling against her mouth.

Later, when the lantern dimmed and the horses settled, Avery pressed her cheek to his shoulder, his heartbeat steady beneath her palm.

For the first time in years, she didn't feel broken.

She felt chosen.

And for once… she wasn't scared of the fall.

Logan's POV

Logan Hunter woke the same way he'd fallen asleep — with Avery in his arms and trouble in his chest.

The fire had burned low, leaving the room dim and warm, but the heat pressed against his front wasn't from the flames. It was from her — all soft curves and slow breathing, tucked against him like she belonged there. Like she'd been there long before last night.

He'd slept with women before.

He'd woken up beside women before.

But never like this.

Never with a knot in his throat and his hand already drifting to her waist, making sure she was real. Never with the fierce, bone-deep thought that if she tried to leave, he'd pull her right back where she was now.

Avery shifted in her sleep, her breath catching as she pressed closer. He swallowed hard, every muscle tightening. "Careful, Doc…" he whispered, rough with sleep. "I might get ideas."

He didn't miss the way her pulse fluttered under his arm.

She was thinking — overthinking — he could practically feel it. She always did. Her thoughts pulsed through her like a heartbeat. She was already convincing herself this meant less than it did. That what happened last night was something she could fold neatly away and ignore.

Hell no.

He'd held her through the storm, through her shaking breaths, through the moment she whispered his name like it meant something — and he wasn't about to pretend it didn't.

He wasn't walking away.

She'd burrowed into him when the wind outside roared loud enough to shake the cabin. She'd kissed him like she was drowning and he was air. She'd fallen asleep right here, head on his chest, trusting him to keep the world out.

The ache that hit him now wasn't lust.

It was possession.

Mine.

The word slipped through his mind before he could stop it. Dangerous. Foolish. True.

Avery murmured something under her breath and he froze.

Did she hear him?

Did he say it out loud?

Her lashes fluttered. She was waking up.

He shut his eyes, pretending he'd been asleep the whole time, but his arm tightened around her instinctively, pulling her in before she could slip away.

"Your thoughts are showing, Doc," he rasped when she fully stirred.

She jolted slightly. He felt the embarrassment ripple through her — felt her try to pull back, to retreat into safety. Into distance.

He wasn't letting her do that.

Not after last night.

He propped himself up, letting his eyes roam over her messy hair and the blanket half-slipping off her shoulder. Beautiful. Frustrating. His.

"You were supposed to be asleep," she breathed.

"No chance of that," he muttered. "Not with you squirming around like you're planning an escape."

She flushed. God, that blush. It hit him like a punch every time. "I wasn't—"

"Yeah," he said softly, "you were."

He shifted out of bed before he did something reckless, like drag her back down and kiss her until she admitted she felt everything he felt. Pancakes. He could hide behind pancakes. Maybe.

She padded behind him, wrapped in a blanket, watching him like she wasn't sure what to make of him in daylight — shirtless, barefoot, domestic.

He caught her staring.

Couldn't help teasing.

"Keep looking at me like that and I'm gonna burn the whole damn kitchen," he smirked.

She flushed deeper. Good. He liked being the one to do that to her.

Breakfast passed in comfortable silence, but inside, he was a mess of thoughts he couldn't say aloud.

When she talked about her clinic — the women she helped, the pain she eased, the battles she fought — something inside him settled. He knew how to fix fences and deliver calves and break wild horses. But what she did? That was real work. Hard work. Brave work.

And when she asked if he wanted to see it, he didn't hesitate.

Of course he did.

Watching her in the clinic, talking to patients, moving with confidence, smoothing worry from people's faces — it hit him in a way he wasn't prepared for.

Pride.

Admiration.

Want.

One of the nurses teased them and he didn't mind. Hell, he liked it. Being seen as hers.

And when Avery muttered "You make everyone fall for you a little," he almost stopped breathing.

Everyone?

No.

Just her.

Driving home, he looked at her profile — the curve of her jaw, the way she twisted her hands in her lap when she was nervous — and knew he'd fallen first. Hard.

Later, in the barn — their barn — he watched her from a distance as she traced the stall door with her fingers. The light hit her hair just right. She looked like she belonged there, like this ranch had been waiting for her all along.

"You looked good today," he said before he could think.

Good.

Confident.

Mine.

When she asked where she belonged with him… he nearly told her. All of it. Too soon. Too much.

Instead, he cupped her jaw, slow and gentle, like she was something precious.

She shook. Said it was cold.

He knew better.

"You feel it too, don't you?" he whispered.

The shift.

The danger.

The truth.

When she whispered Logan… in that voice — soft, uncertain, wanting — he almost broke.

Then the kiss happened — slow, deep, honest —
and he knew he was done for. Completely.

Avery Collins wasn't just a woman he was helping.

Wasn't just a fake wife in a fake marriage.

She was the first real thing he'd felt in years.

And as she curled into him again, pressing her face
against his neck, he tightened his hold around her
instinctively.

"Mine," he whispered into her hair.

This time he knew she didn't hear.

But he meant every word.

Chapter 14

Secrets In The Dark

The storm had passed, leaving the ranch sparkling under a pale winter sun. Avery lingered in the kitchen, her hands wrapped around a mug of coffee, watching the frost glitter on the windows. The cabin was quiet—almost too quiet—but that was exactly how she liked it when Logan was around.

He emerged from the barn, dusting snow off his jacket, hair mussed by the wind. The way the sunlight hit his broad shoulders made her heart skip, and she found herself lingering on the curve of his jaw, the hint of stubble that begged for her fingers.

"Morning, beautiful," he drawled, voice low, teasing—but carrying a weight she couldn't ignore.

"Morning," she replied, a flutter in her chest. "You look like you survived a snowstorm out there."

"Barely," he said, shrugging, but there was a grin tugging at the corner of his mouth. "I had to come check on my favorite surgeon."

Avery laughed softly, sipping her coffee. "I didn't know you were that concerned about my heart rate in the morning."

"More than your heart rate," he said, stepping closer, every movement deliberate. "I care about the part of you that doesn't tell me what it's thinking."

She swallowed, heat pooling in her chest. His words always carried a quiet authority, a magnetic pull that made her want to lean in closer—even when she knew it was dangerous.

They moved toward the living room. Logan settled into his usual spot by the fire, stretching his long legs, and Avery mirrored him, slipping onto the couch with the mug still in her hands. They sat in companionable silence for a moment, the crackle of the flames filling the space.

Finally, Logan's voice broke the quiet. "I know what you're like at the clinic—steady, calm, saving everyone who walks through the door. But the hospital… you don't say much about it. I don't really know what it asks of you."

Avery blinked, surprised by the interest. Most people didn't want to hear about the long hours, the pressure, the lives on the line. But Logan… he leaned forward slightly, elbows resting on his knees, watching her like he actually wanted to know.

"I'm a surgeon," she said finally, choosing her words carefully. "It's… intense. Long hours, high stakes. You get used to the adrenaline, the pressure, the constant need to be perfect."

He nodded, eyes dark and intent. "And you handle it all. Every day?"

"I try," she admitted. "Sometimes I don't. Sometimes it's… exhausting." Her fingers tightened around the mug. "I enjoy fixing things, saving people—but it's difficult. And sometimes, you feel the weight of every mistake, even when it's not yours."

Logan's hand brushed hers as he reached to take a sip from his own cup. "Sounds like you carry a lot," he whispered. "But that's why I admire you. You don't hide from the hard stuff. You face it."

Avery's chest tightened. His admiration was effortless, quiet, not over-the-top. He didn't need to flaunt it—he made her feel seen. And that feeling… it scared her as much as it thrilled her.

They fell into a peaceful rhythm, the kind that felt almost dangerous in how comfortable it was.

Avery told him about the little boy who'd swallowed a marble and insisted it made him a superhero. "He called it his 'power stone,'" she said, laughing softly. "When I told him it would come out the other end, he said, 'Good. Then I'll have powers in both directions.'"

Logan's laugh rumbled through the quiet kitchen. "Kid's got spirit. Reminds me of my nephew—he broke his arm trying to ride a calf like a bull. Said he was training for the rodeo."

She smiled, tracing the rim of her mug. "Kids bounce back faster than adults. It's the grown-ups who break and pretend they don't."

He nodded, something flickering in his eyes. "Yeah. I've seen that too."

The conversation shifted. She told him about a rough night in the OR—how a young mother had coded three times before they got her back. "You'd think saving someone like that would make you feel powerful," she said quietly, "but mostly you just feel small, and lucky, and scared it'll happen again."

Logan didn't interrupt. He just reached across the table and covered her hand with his calloused thumb brushing her knuckles. "You keep people alive," he said. "Don't sell that short."

For a moment, the only sound was the ticking of the old clock above the stove.

Then Avery cleared her throat, smiling again. "Okay, lighter story," she said. "There was this old rancher who refused anesthesia because he wanted to 'watch the show.' I told him we don't let an audience into surgery, and he said, 'Well, I'm payin' for it, ain't I?'"

Logan's grin returned, slow and warm. "That sounds like every man over fifty in this county."

They laughed together, the kind of laughter that came easy, and every so often, their hands brushed—a fleeting touch that sent shivers racing through her.

At one point, he leaned back, smirking. "So when you're saving lives in that hospital, do you ever think about someone stuck in a snowstorm, waiting to be saved in a more… domestic setting?"

Avery rolled her eyes but couldn't hide the blush that warmed her cheeks. "I think about making sure the person sitting next to me doesn't die from frostbite first."

"Good," he murmured, leaning closer until their knees touched. "Because I plan to survive… only if you're monitoring me."

The tension between them built slowly, quietly, each glance and brush of skin charged with unspoken desire. They knew each other in ways that transcended words—what had started as flirtation, teasing, and playful banter had transformed into something deeper, something that neither of them could deny anymore.

As the afternoon waned, Logan stretched and tilted his head toward the window. "You've been talking all morning. Let's take a break. Come outside with me."

Avery hesitated, glancing at the sun-dappled snow. "Outside? In the cold?"

"Exactly," he said, smirking. "You can tell me how a doctor survives a winter storm without losing her mind."

She laughed, slipping into her coat, gloves, and boots. The crisp air bit at her cheeks, but it was invigorating. Logan fell into step beside her as they ventured toward the paddocks, the snow crunching softly under their feet.

"I never realized how much work goes into keeping this place running," she said, brushing snow off the fence post. "I see you out here all the time, but being fully involved… it's different."

Logan chuckled, leaning against the rail. "It's not glamorous. Just like your work. But I wanted you to see it the way I see it—hands on, all of it. You know, the things I care about."

Avery tilted her head, studying him. "Is this your way of showing off?" she teased.

"Maybe," he drawled, eyes darkening. "Or maybe I just want you to understand a part of me the way I understand you. Your work… your life… It's impressive, Avery. And I don't just mean the surgeries."

Her heart stuttered. She had been so used to being the one in control, the one saving lives, that having someone genuinely admire her… and notice her… was intoxicating.

Avery followed Logan along the fence-line, her boots crunching over the packed snow. The sky hung low and gray, the kind of winter light that turned everything silver. He moved a few paces ahead, shoulders broad beneath his flannel and jacket, every motion steady and sure.

"Post's loose," he said, crouching to test it. "You wanna hand me that hammer?"

Avery picked it up, only for it to slide from her gloves and bounce off the post before disappearing into the snow.

Logan let out a low laugh. "Careful there. I ain't lookin' to spend my afternoon dodgin' tools."

She shot him a glare, though the heat in her cheeks gave her away. "It slipped."

He smirked. "Sure it did."

Logan glanced up. "You're learnin'. " You can't expect a city girl to fix a fence on her first day out."

"Hey, I can handle more than you think," she shot back. "I just rarely do it in the snow."

He chuckled low, the sound warm against the cold air. "You'll get used to it. Wyoming doesn't stop for weather—or for people who'd rather stay inside."

She rolled her eyes. "Noted, cowboy."

"Cowboy, huh?" He straightened, tapping the hammer against the post. "Thought we were on a first-name basis now."

She smiled despite herself. "Fine, Logan. Better?"

He tipped his hat, grin widening. "Much."

They moved down the fence line, replacing a few nails and checking latches. A group of horses watched from the pasture, breath misting like smoke. When one of them nosed her shoulder, Avery laughed softly and ran her hand down its neck.

"She likes you," Logan said, watching her.

"She likes the hay I dropped," Avery said, pretending not to notice the way his gaze lingered.

He walked closer, brushing his gloved hand over the horse's mane. "Still. She rarely lets strangers touch her."

Avery looked up at him. "Guess I'm not a stranger anymore then."

For a heartbeat, he didn't move. Just studied her, eyes flicking from hers to her lips before he looked away. "Guess not," he whispered.

Snowflakes drifted between them, catching on the brim of his hat, on her lashes. The world felt smaller in that moment—quiet, except for the creak of the fence and the low breath of the horses.

Logan finally cleared his throat. "You ever mucked a stall before?"

Her nose wrinkled. "Can't say that I have."

He grinned. "Well, there's a first time for everything."

She groaned, but followed him into the barn. The scent of hay and earth was stronger there, warm against the chill. He showed her how to shovel and spread fresh straw, teasing her when she nearly tripped over a bucket.

"Don't laugh," she said, trying to balance the pitchfork.

"Can't help it," he said, voice rough with amusement. "You're fightin' that shovel like it insulted you."

"I'm doing fine," she huffed.

"You're doin' somethin'," he said with a smirk. "Fine might be generous."

She threw him a mock glare, but when their eyes met again, the laughter faded into something softer. The air between them hummed. When they finally stepped back outside, the sun was dipping low, painting the snow in gold. Avery's breath came out in clouds, her cheeks pink from the cold and the quiet warmth of being near him.

"Didn't realize ranch work came with this kind of view," she said.

Logan looked out over the land, then at her. "Yeah," he murmured. "Sometimes it's worth the work."

The light waned, casting long shadows over the paddocks. Logan paused, leaning against the railing, letting the silence hang between them.
 "Do you ever think about… everything we did yesterday?" His voice was low, rough with something that wasn't quite restrained.

Avery swallowed hard, cheeks warming.
"Sometimes. I… I can't stop thinking about it."

He stepped closer, close enough that she could feel the heat radiating off him, the scent of cedar and leather surrounding them.
 "Good," he murmured. "Because I haven't stopped thinking either."

They lingered in the snow, the quiet between them charged with anticipation. Avery wanted to speak, to confess how she felt, but the words caught in her throat. Logan, sensing her hesitation, brushed a lock of hair from her face, thumb tracing the line of her cheek.

"You've got snow in your hair," he breathed.

"Guess that's what happens when you work outside all day," she replied, smiling faintly.

He laughed under his breath, the sound low and rough. "You complain a lot less than your family said."

Avery froze, the smile faltering. The memory of her parents' laughter, the offhand jokes about her "never finishing anything," flickered through her mind.

Logan must've seen something in her face, because his voice softened. "They were wrong, you know. You don't quit easy."

She swallowed hard, eyes dropping to the snow at their feet. "You didn't have to defend me that night."

"Yeah," he said quietly, "I did."

The words hung between them, heavier than the cold air, warmer than she expected.

Logan broke the silence first, nodding toward the barn. "Come on. Still got to get the horses settled before dark."

She followed, grateful for the distraction, though her heartbeat didn't slow. The air inside the barn was warmer, filled with the scent of hay and pine. Logan moved easily among the stalls, checking latches and tossing feed. She watched him in the dim light—the quiet competence of his movements, the way his presence filled the space without effort.

"Hand me that brush, would you?" he asked over his shoulder.

She passed it to him, fingers grazing his. The touch was brief, but it sent another shiver through her. He caught her gaze, and neither of them looked away this time.

"Thanks," he said, voice softer now.

Avery nodded, setting the brush aside. Her gaze drifted along the wall of tools—bridles, leads, coils of rope hung in neat loops. She didn't mean to stare, but something about the order of it all—the control, the care—made her linger a little too long.

When she looked back, Logan was watching her. Not judging, not teasing, just watching, his expression unreadable.

"You okay?" he asked quietly.

"Yeah," she said quickly, forcing a small smile. "Just... thinking."

He held her gaze for a beat longer than necessary, then nodded once and turned back to the horses. "You think too much, Collins."

Avery smiled faintly, but her pulse didn't ease. The horses shifted behind them, the steady rhythm of their breathing the only sound. Snow tapped lightly against the barn roof.

For a moment, it felt like the world had narrowed to this—just them, the quiet, and everything unsaid.

Logan cleared his throat and set the brush aside. "We should head in," he said finally. "Cold's getting to you."

She hesitated. "You sure it's the cold?"

His mouth curved into the faintest smile. "No," he said. "But that's the excuse I'm usin'."

He moved to hang the brush on the wall, but didn't turn back right away. His shoulders rose and fell with a slow breath, as if he were weighing something.

"When I was younger," he said quietly, still facing the stall door, "I used to ride in rodeos."

Avery blinked. "You? I didn't picture you as the adrenaline junkie type."

He turned then, a crooked smile ghosting his lips. "Yeah, well. I thought I was bulletproof back then. Papaw used to say I was born with more grit than sense."

He paused, the faintest edge of memory tightening his jaw. "Last bull I rode was called *Hollow's Ghost.* Fitting name, I guess. I lost my core halfway through—leaned forward when I should've leaned back. Took a horn straight to the jaw, then got head-butted clean into the dirt. Broke three ribs, my collarbone, and a couple teeth for good measure."

Avery's breath caught. "Logan…"

He gave a small shrug, the movement careful. "Doc said I was lucky to walk away. Papaw sat by my bed two days straight, just kept pourin' coffee and starin' out the window. When I finally came to, he said, 'The ground's got a hard way of teachin' you what matters.'"

His voice dropped lower. "I didn't argue. Sold my gear, came home, and figured maybe the land was enough of a fight."

For a moment, the only sound was the wind sliding along the barn roof and the soft snort of a horse nearby. Avery watched him, the way his eyes stayed fixed on the floorboards like he was still seeing that arena—dust, noise, pain.

She stepped closer, her hand brushing his arm. "That must've been hard. Walking away."

He met her gaze, something unguarded flickering behind the blue. "Yeah. But I'd already broken what needed breakin'. The rest wasn't worth losing."

Avery's throat tightened. "And you never went back?"

He shook his head. "No. Sometimes I miss the ride, the rush. But I've got different reasons to wake up before sunrise now."

Her lips curved softly. "Like chickens and frozen fences?"

He laughed quietly, the sound low and rough. "Among other things."

For a heartbeat, they stood close enough that her breath fogged against his coat. The firelight from the house glowed faintly through the frosted window, painting the edges of his face in gold. There was a steadiness in him she hadn't noticed before—a peace born from surviving what should've finished him.

Avery found herself whispering, "You really loved it, didn't you?"

Logan nodded once. "Yeah. But I love what I've got now more."

They lingered there longer than they meant to, the quiet stretching between them until the wind howled again outside the barn doors…

The walk back to the house was slow. The last traces of sunlight faded behind the hills, the air sharp with the smell of woodsmoke. Neither of them spoke. Every step seemed to pull the silence tighter, until the creak of the porch boards sounded louder than it should have.

Inside, the fire still glowed low in the hearth. Logan shut the door behind them, the sound echoing through the quiet house. Avery shrugged off her coat, the warmth of the room wrapping around her.

He moved closer, eyes never leaving hers. "You warm enough?"

She nodded, though her pulse said otherwise.

Sometimes, when the fire caught her just right, he thought Avery looked like sunlight poured into motion — all warmth and strength and something he couldn't name without falling a little further.

Logan reached out, brushing his fingers lightly against her wrist. "Good," he murmured. "'Cause I've got a feeling we're not done talkin' yet."

Avery's breath caught. "Talkin', huh?" she said, her voice softer than she intended.

Logan's mouth curved, a slow, knowing grin. "That's one word for it."

He moved past her, tossing another log into the fire. Sparks leapt, casting his face in gold and shadow. Avery's eyes followed the motion—the flex of his shoulders beneath his flannel, the slow ease of him in his own skin. He wasn't trying to be anything. He just *was*. And that, somehow, was worse.

"You're starin'," he drawled without looking up.

Her cheeks warmed. "You make it hard not to."

That got his attention. He turned, eyes dark and unreadable. "Careful, sweetheart. You start talkin' like that, and I might think you mean it."

"Maybe I do."

Silence. The kind that hummed, thick and charged. He took a step closer, then another, until she could see the small flecks of green in his eyes.

"Say it again," he said quietly.

Her voice faltered, but she didn't look away. "Maybe I do."

He studied her for a long moment, the muscle in his jaw ticking. "You got no idea what you're doin' to me, do you?"

She smiled, small but certain. "I think I do."

Logan exhaled slowly, the sound almost a growl. "Avery…"

Her name came out rough, warning and wanting all at once. She felt it like a shiver straight through her.

The fire popped, and the house seemed to shrink around them. Every breath, every heartbeat filled the space between them. Logan reached up, brushing his thumb across her bottom lip, slow enough for her to stop him—but she didn't.

He exhaled, eyes dark with something unreadable, then stepped back a fraction and gave a crooked grin. "We oughta find somethin' to take our minds off all this starin'."

Avery blinked, trying to steady her pulse. "Like what?"

He glanced toward the small table by the fire. "Cards."

"Cards?" she echoed, half-laughing.

"Yeah," he said, already reaching for a deck sitting on the shelf. "Poker. Simple keeps a man honest."

"Honest?" she teased, recovering a little. "That doesn't sound like you."

He chuckled, shuffling the cards with lazy confidence. "You wound me, Doc. Tell you what—how 'bout we make it interestin'? Losers take a penalty."

She folded her arms, suspicious. "What kind of penalty?"

"I don't know yet." His eyes glinted in the firelight. "Guess we'll figure that out when you lose."

"Pretty sure you're overestimating yourself, cowboy."

He grinned wider. "All right then, deal you in?"

She sighed, giving in with a smile. "Fine. But I want fair stakes."

"Fair?" he echoed, pretending to think. "Loser sheds a layer. Keeps the odds even."

Avery's laugh came out half-nervous, half-amused. "You're kidding."

"Wouldn't dream of it," he said, sliding the first cards her way. "Sides, you look like you could use a way to warm up."

She shook her head, smiling despite herself. "You're trouble."

"Darlin', you have no idea."

The cards snapped on the table; the firelight flickering between them, and just like that, the air shifted again—still warm, still playful, but humming with that same unspoken energy neither of them wanted to name.

Avery held her cards close, biting back a grin. "You sure you want to do this? I play to win."

Logan smirked, leaning back in his chair. "So do I."

They played a few rounds, the sound of cards and laughter mixing with the soft crackle of the fire. Avery tried to keep her poker face, but Logan's stare made it impossible to focus. He was too relaxed, too confident, too—*him*.

After her first win, she tilted her head, savoring the look on his face. "Well?"

He sighed dramatically, tugging off his jacket and tossing it over the chair. "Don't get too proud. That was beginner's luck."

"Pretty sure that was skill," she shot back.

"Skill, huh?" He started dealing again, slow and deliberate. "Let's test that theory."

Avery narrowed her eyes. "You're bluffing already."

"Maybe," he said, that lazy grin never faltering. "You'll just have to find out the hard way."

The next round went fast. Avery lost—and groaned when Logan raised an eyebrow toward her sweater.

"Oh, come on. That hardly seems fair."

"Fair's what we agreed on," he said, voice dripping with amusement. "Unless you're quittin'."

"Never."

She pulled the sweater over her head, leaving her in a thin tank top. Logan's gaze flickered briefly—quick, but not unnoticed.

"What?" she challenged.

"Just surprised, that's all," he said, tone light but eyes darker than before. "Didn't figure the doc had a competitive streak this mean."

"Guess you don't know me as well as you think."

Round after round went by—each one closer, riskier. As the pile of clothes on the chair grew, the distance between them shrank. Logan's laughter came easier now, low and genuine. Avery's cheeks burned, but her smile wouldn't fade.

When she leaned forward to throw her next card, her knee brushed his under the table. Neither of them moved away.

"Seems like you're distracted," he murmured.

"Maybe I'm just enjoying watching you lose."

He chuckled, slow and rough. "Careful, sweetheart. You keep talkin' like that, I'll have to win on purpose."

"Pretty sure you're trying to already."

"Maybe." He leaned forward, elbows on the table, closing the space between them. "Maybe I just like seein' how far you'll push your luck."

The air thickened. Firelight danced between them, the soft glow catching the curve of her mouth, the rise of her breath.

His laugh faded, the fire popping once in the quiet. Avery's hand brushed his as she reached for a card—a fleeting touch, but enough to make her chest tighten. Neither of them moved.

"You gonna raise the stakes, doc?" he murmured, leaning just a fraction closer, eyes glinting with challenge.

"Guess you'll have to show me what winning looks like, cowboy," she shot back, her voice a little shaky but daring.

"If I win, then I get to tie you up and have my way with you all night long."

The words hung between them, heavier than any bet they'd made. Logan's gaze flicked from her eyes to her lips and back, slow, deliberate, making her pulse hammer in her ears.

He reached out, brushing a stray card off the table, his fingers lingering across hers. Warm. Electric. The contact made her forget what round they were even playing.

A beat passed. And another.

The firelight flickered across his face, softening the shadows, but his expression was sharp, attentive, waiting for her next move.

Every laugh, every tease, every brush of skin—they'd led here. The game had shifted. The table, the cards, the stakes—they were gone. All that remained was them.

Logan flipped his last card with a confident flick. "Full house," he said, eyes dark and mischievous. "Looks like I win."

Avery's lips curved into a small, daring smile. "Figures."

He leaned forward, letting their hands brush across the table. "You know what that means," he murmured, voice low, teasing.

"I know," she said, heart hammering. Her gaze didn't waver. "You're collecting your winnings."

"Exactly," he said, letting the corner of his mouth twitch into a grin. "And I intend to enjoy every second of it."

Her chest fluttered, anticipation and trust mixing into something delicious. "Then I guess I'll just… have to let you," she whispered, the words playful but certain.

He leaned closer, brushing his fingers along hers again. "Glad we're on the same page."

The tension in the room shifted, thick and charged. Every glance, every touch, every unspoken word promised what was coming next—both of them on the edge, ready, willing, and perfectly matched in this little game of chance.

Logan stood up, walked to the fireplace and grabbed the spare ropes he kept there. Avery's breath caught in her throat.

"You were serious about tying me up?"

"Yes, I won, so I get to have fun," he smirked at her. "Having regrets about agreeing to play?"

"No," she said a little too quickly.

"Good. Do you trust me, Avery?"

"Yes," she said with a slight hesitation.

'Avery, do you trust me?" he said more firmly.

"Yes, Logan," she breathed.

"Good, let's go."

She followed him to the bedroom. As the door closed behind them, her heart rate picked up. Avery was excited but nervous. She had experienced nothing like this before — a man wanted to tie her up and worship her body. *That's what he is going to do, right?* Nerves racked her body, and her anxiety and excitement fought for dominance.

"Get on the bed," he said, voice low enough to vibrate through her. "If you want this the way I think you do."

Surprised, she did as she was told. He had never talked to her like that, but when she looked in his eyes, she knew. His pupils were wide, his stare unrelenting, full of something she couldn't name but felt in every nerve.

Logan kissed her, a deep kiss that made her lose her breath and feel dizzy. As they came up for air, he grabbed each wrist.
His fingers paused at her wrists. "You trust me?"
"Yes."
His gaze darkened. "Then let me have you." He then proceeded to tie both wrists against the headboard.

He kissed her again, moving to her neck and kissing her there. His tongue traced the fading hickeys from two days prior. He marked her again, sucking on her flesh, causing her to moan.

"Now listen up, darlin'. If you ever need me to back off, your safe word is 'Red.' You say it, I stop. Understand?"

Avery *nodded quickly.*

"Words, Avery. Don't just look cute," he said.

"Yes, I understand Red is my safe word," she responded.

Logan *smirks, eyes glinting.* "That's my good girl. Keepin' me honest."

She needed this, to let him have his way with her. Letting go of all control she had, no decisions, no responsibilities, no consequences — just submission.

Logan's fingers trailed over her flesh, causing her nipples to turn into stiff peaks, begging to be touched.

Every time his fingers skimmed close, her breath hitched, her body arching like it couldn't help reaching for him.

"Please," she begged.

Her thighs were already slick with her juices. One of her nipples was in Logan's mouth, while he was toying with the other. Beneath him, she writhed and moaned as his tongue played with her erect nipples.

"For someone who likes being in charge," he growled, "you make a damn perfect little slut when you want to, don't you?"

Avery made a whimper as he squeezed her nipples. Next, he raised each leg. He used the rope to secure her ankles, widening her legs so he could see everything.

Her folds were slick with her juices, and he could see it all.

"Do you remember your safe word, Avery?" he asked, slipping his hand between her thighs.

"Yes," she cried as he slid his fingers through her wet folds. Circling his finger over her clit, he teased her.

Logan knelt between her thighs, exhaling like the sight of her alone knocked the wind out of him.

Avery's breath caught, anticipating what was about to happen. She had never had a man eat her out before, and he was doing it again, like it was his favorite meal.

His tongue was warm when he flattened it against her core, causing her to moan loudly.

"Logan," she breathed breathlessly.

He wasted no time sucking and flicking his tongue over her sensitive bundle of nerves repeatedly. He sucked on her clit while using two fingers to penetrate her. As he thrust into her, he could feel her body beginning to tense up. He then curled his fingers inside her as he continued to thrust into her, hitting her G-spot over and over while continuing his torture on her clit.

She tried to pull away from him; the sensation was too much, but she didn't want him to stop. Logan grabbed both of her thighs and wrapped his arms around them, holding her in place. Avery screamed so loud it seemed as if she shook the walls of the house. Her whole body bowed, the orgasm ripping through her so sharply she cried out his name. Logan took his time lapping up every single drop from her body. She jerked as he passed his tongue one last time over her sensitive clit.

Logan rose, looking down at her trembling body. He kissed her lips, making her taste herself. Logan untied her ankles.

He flipped her onto her stomach with a grip that was firm but careful, giving her a second to breathe before he stripped off his boxers.
"Still with me, Avery?"
"Yes," she breathed.
"Good."

He slid behind her, pressing the hot length of him against her soaked center. He rubbed the tip of his cock up and down her slit, spreading her arousal. Logan smacked her ass hard. Avery groaned in response, pushing her ass back into him. He smacked her again. He then thrust forward, no warning, no restrained, just rough and hard as she had needed.

"Yes, Logan, harder please," she begged.

He groaned, "Darlin', reckon you're gonna be the death of me."

He fucked her relentlessly with no mercy. She threw her ass back at him. Making him hit her in that spot that made her go wild. This wasn't a tender kind of loving. It was hard, fast and dirty and everything she needed and more. Logan grabbed her hair, pulling her head back as he fucked her roughly. This was raunchy sex she never knew existed. Logan was about to come when felt her walls squeeze him.

Right then and there he knew she was close to another orgasm.

"Cum for me, baby."

Avery's body did as she was told as if he owned her.

They came together, Avery milking him of every drop he had to give.

"Jesus, darlin'… every time I think I've had my fill of you, you ruin me all over again."

Avery, too tired to respond, just made a barely audible sound. He chuckled. Realizing he had left her speechless. He then untied her wrist rubbing them to bring the blood flow back there.

Afterward, they remained in the bed; the fire crackled softly. Avery curled against Logan, resting her head on his chest, tracing lazy patterns across his arm. He held her with an ease that was both comforting and electrifying.

"You know," she murmured, voice barely above a whisper, "I never thought being trapped here would feel like… this."

Logan's hand threaded through her hair. "Neither did I," he admitted. "But I'm glad we were."

They spoke in whispers then, sharing secrets neither had told anyone else—past heartbreaks, small fears, moments of weakness. Logan confessed the first time he had ever lost someone he loved, and how it had left him questioning everything about trust. Avery revealed insecurities about her PCOS, about the pressure she felt to always succeed, about her fear of being truly seen.

Each revelation deepened the connection between them. They held each other tighter, the boundaries between physical desire and emotional intimacy blurring. Every sigh, every soft touch, carried both reassurance and longing.

As night settled outside, Avery realized that in Logan's presence, she could be completely vulnerable. And for the first time, she allowed herself to truly believe someone could see all of her—and still want her.

The fire burned lower, their breaths mingling in the quiet cabin. Logan's voice, low and gentle, broke the silence. "Whatever this is… whatever we are… I want you to know I'm not going anywhere."

Avery closed her eyes, letting his words sink in, feeling the warmth of the cabin, the storm outside, and the undeniable bond forming between them.

And in the quiet darkness, she whispered back,
"Neither am I."

Chapter 15

Heated Interruptions

The morning sun filtered weakly through frost-covered cabin windows, casting a pale glow over the bedroom. Avery stretched, still wrapped in the warmth of the blankets, her head resting against Logan's chest. The quiet hum of the heating stove and the faint creak of the cabin settling made the world feel impossibly intimate, like it belonged only to them.

Logan's fingers traced lazy circles on the back of her hand, his thumb brushing her knuckles in a rhythm that had her pulse quickening despite the calm morning. She tilted her head, meeting his gaze. The firelight danced across his features, making his eyes look darker, sharper, more magnetic than ever.

"You know," he murmured, voice low and rough, "I could get used to mornings like this."

Avery smiled, a soft warmth spreading through her chest. "And I could get used to someone making me coffee in bed," she teased, though her heart was still racing.

He chuckled, the sound vibrating against her skin. "Coffee can wait," he said, leaning down to brush a kiss over her temple, then the corner of her mouth. Every touch was deliberate, slow, designed to tease.

Avery's breath hitched slightly. "Oh, really?" she whispered, a mischievous gleam in her eyes. "And what exactly would you do while coffee waits?"

Logan's gaze darkened just a fraction, a low, playful growl in his voice. "I reckon… I'd eat you for breakfast."

A shiver ran through her at the words, and before she could tease him back, his hand slid to the small of her back, pulling her closer. Fingers traced lazy patterns along her spine, and she pressed herself against him, laughing softly as he nipped at her earlobe.

"You're insufferable," she murmured, breathless but smiling, sliding her fingers along his forearm, teasing a reaction.

"Only for you," he whispered, lips brushing against her hairline, fingers curling gently in her curls. "Just try and tell me you don't like it."

Avery tilted her head, catching his gaze, their noses nearly touching, pulses racing, laughter mingling with soft sighs. The cabin felt impossibly small, the morning sun weak through frost-covered windows, the world outside fading to nothing but the two of them.

Then—**crunch, crunch**—boots on the porch froze them both.

A cheerful voice called from the doorway. "Hello? Anyone home? We brought breakfast!"

Avery groaned, hiding her face in the crook of Logan's neck. "Family," she muttered.

Logan pressed a kiss to her temple, smirking. "Guess our private morning isn't going to be so private."

They quickly got dressed and headed to open the front door for her family.

The door swung open, revealing Avery's parents and brother, bundled in winter coats, cheeks pink from the cold. Their smiles were warm, oblivious to the tension that had filled the room only moments ago.

"Good morning!" her mother said brightly. "We finally made it back—turns out that storm had us snowed in at the ski resort overnight. They upgraded us to a luxury suite while we waited it out.

Honestly, we could've stayed forever. We're just stopping by before heading back up there again."

Avery's father glanced at Logan and gave him a nod of greeting, completely unaware of the effect the couple's closeness had had just seconds before.

Logan stood, adjusting his jacket with effortless grace, though his dark gaze lingered on Avery. He let her slip out of his arms just enough to answer her parents, though every subtle movement, every brush of his hand as he gestured, was deliberate—reminding Avery of their connection.

They moved through breakfast with polite conversation. Avery's parents chatted about ski conditions, Avery's brother teased about who would fall first on the slopes, and Logan answered questions with his usual charm. But every so often, his hand would find hers under the table, just for a second, and Avery's pulse would spike.

"You two look cozy," her brother teased. "Storm keeping you up?"

Logan shrugged, deadpan. "Storm. Drafty cabin. A lot of noise."

Avery elbowed him. "Logan."

"What?" he said innocently. "I'm talkin' about the WEATHER."

Her brother laughed. Avery wanted to die.

After breakfast, her parents stepped outside to admire the snowy pasture. Avery and Logan followed, their boots crunching in the fresh powder. The air was crisp, biting at their cheeks, but the proximity to each other kept their warmth.

As they reached the paddocks, Logan leaned close, brushing a strand of hair from her face. "Still want to finish our discussion from this morning?" he murmured, his lips brushing her ear.

Avery bit back a laugh, heat pooling in her chest. "I think we need more privacy for that," she whispered.

"Privacy, huh?" he said, dark eyes flicking toward the snow-laden barn. "We could improvise…"

Before anything else could happen, Avery's mother's voice carried from the edge of the field. "Avery! Come see the chickens!"

Avery groaned, glancing at Logan. He only smirked, the teasing sparkle in his eyes matching her own rising frustration. "Family. Always the perfect interruption," he muttered while brushing snow from her coat.

Despite the repeated interruptions, they found stolen moments—fingers brushing while carrying hay, a shoulder touching a hip as they worked to corral the animals, laughter shared quietly at the absurdity of being interrupted by family mid-desire. Every glance, every touch, carried the unspoken promise of more.

Avery felt him before she saw him—solid heat at her back, a presence that made her pulse trip over itself. She kept her hands on the gate, pretending to adjust the latch, pretending not to notice how close Logan was standing.

But he stepped closer anyway. Just close enough that his chest brushed her shoulder. Just close enough she could feel his breath hit the shell of her ear.

"You keep bendin' like that," he murmured, voice low enough only she could hear, "and I'm gonna forget your whole damn family is ten feet away."

Her fingers froze, breath catching in her throat.

"Logan—" she whispered.

"Mhm." His lips didn't touch her ear, but she felt every syllable shiver down her spine. "Say my name any softer and they're all gonna know exactly what I'm thinkin'."

She swallowed hard, trying to keep her movements neutral, normal—family-friendly. He leaned one hand on the fence beside her hip, looking like he was simply helping…but he dipped his head just enough so that only she could hear him.

"You don't know what you look like right now," he said, voice slow and dark. "Tryin' so hard to look innocent while you're drivin' me outta my damn mind."

Her knees wobbled. She steadied herself on the gate.

"You keep movin' like that," he went on, "and I'm gonna be thinkin' about takin' you around the corner of this barn where they can't see."

His hand brushed her lower back—barely a touch, but it nearly melted her.

"And trust me, darlin'… you wouldn't be fixin' fences anymore."

Avery sucked in a breath way too sharp.

Logan didn't smirk, didn't look at her—just adjusted the gate like nothing happened.

But under his breath, only for her:

"You're killin' me tryin' to behave."

And then louder, perfectly casual for her family to hear:

"That gate's good. Nice and sturdy."

Avery almost collapsed.

As the sun dipped behind the horizon, casting molten gold across the barn, Avery and Logan found a rare sliver of quiet. The animals were settled, the field empty, the world soft and unmoving.

Avery's gaze drifted to the neatly coiled rope hanging from a post.

Her pulse jumped.

Logan saw it — and the slow, dark curl of his smile told her he knew exactly what memory hit her.

"Thinkin' about last night, darlin'?" he murmured, voice thick velvet.

Avery stepped closer, the barn suddenly too warm. "Maybe I am."

His fingers brushed her wrist — barely a touch, but devastating — tracing the rope without taking it.

"Careful," he warned softly. "You're lookin' at that rope like you want me to start somethin' I won't be able to stop."

"Maybe I do," she whispered, breath already unsteady.

Logan moved in until her back touched the post, his body a wall of heat in front of her. One hand slipped to her hip, his thumb dragging lazily along her side, testing how fast she'd come undone.

The rope looped loosely around her wrist — no tension, just memory, just promise.

"You trust me?" he murmured against her jaw.

"Always."

That single word broke something in him.

He leaned in, lips brushing her ear, his voice a molten, barely-controlled whisper that hit like a punch:

"Darlin'… if we weren't one wrong breath away from gettin' caught, I'd have you against this post beggin' me to keep goin'… and you know damn well you'd let me."

Avery's knees nearly buckled — actually buckled — and she grabbed his shirt to stay upright.

Logan's breath hitched at the feel of her clinging to him.

He wasn't smirking anymore.

He looked ruined.

Starving.

His forehead pressed to her cheek, his voice a ragged confession:

"God help me… I'm this close to not carin' who's outside."

Her fingers curled in his jacket. "Logan…"

He was leaning in — not kissing yet, but about to, absolutely about to, the rope sliding through his fingers as his hand found her waist—

CREAK.

The barn door opened.

They froze.

Avery jerked back, breathless and flushed, trying to laugh but sounding wrecked.

Logan stared at the door like it had personally ruined his life.

Under his breath, dark and murderous:

"Swear to God, I'm takin' that door off its hinges."

Logan's hand lingered near hers, palm brushing lightly as they returned to the chores. Every glance, every brush of skin, every unspoken word hung between them, the rope, the teasing, and the anticipation lingering like a spark ready to ignite.

After their playful teasing, they remained in the quiet barn, leaning against the hay bales, fingers occasionally brushing, hands lingering just a little too long. Logan's thumb traced lazy circles over her wrist, brushing her skin in a slow, deliberate rhythm, eyes locked on hers with that same dark, mischievous glint. Neither spoke, but the charged silence between them said everything—they didn't need words to acknowledge the pull, the anticipation, or the promise of what was still to come.

"You're impossible," Avery murmured, but there was no bite in her tone—only a soft warmth.

"I'm impossible?" he teased, leaning close enough that his lips brushed hers. "Or irresistible?"

She laughed softly, pressing closer, warmth pooling between them. "Both," she admitted.

The sun dipped fully behind the mountains, and the cabin lights twinkled in the distance. They lingered a moment longer, holding each other, letting the quiet of the ranch and the snow-filled air wrap around them like a cocoon.

Even with interruptions, even with teasing and laughter, Avery knew one thing: the tension between them wasn't going anywhere. It was growing, smoldering beneath the surface, ready to ignite again at the slightest touch—or glance.

Even after her parents disappeared down the snowy path, Avery's body still thrummed with the leftover heat of Logan's whisper in the barn. Every nerve felt awake. Hyper-aware. Aching.

She tried to focus on the cold air, on the chores, but it was useless.

Logan watched her like he could feel every thought she was trying to push away.

"You're distracted," he murmured, stepping close enough that his chest brushed her shoulder. The touch was subtle — but deliberate. "Real distracted."

She swallowed, attempting a casual shrug through the sudden tightness in her chest. "Maybe I'm cold."

His breath brushed the side of her face. "Sweetheart… you're burnin' up."

Avery turned toward him — mistake.

He was close.

Too close.

Cedar and leather and heat wrapped around her like a hand at her waist.

"You're gonna make this barn dangerous," she whispered, voice trembling in a way she couldn't hide.

Logan's smile was slow and sinful.

"I think you like dangerous."

He brushed a knuckle down the inside of her wrist, pretending to reach for a brush, but his fingers lingered — testing her pulse, feeling the speed of it.

Her breath caught.

"You feel that?" he murmured.

"Logan…"

"That's not cold."

His voice dropped to something dark, something barely held in.

"That's you thinkin' about what I almost did back there."

Her knees wobbled. She grabbed the stall rail to steady herself — which only made his smirk deepen.

"You okay?" he asked softly, stepping even closer. "Or you need me to hold you up?"

"That's not fair," she whispered.

"No," he agreed, leaning in until their noses almost brushed. "But neither is what you do to me."

Avery's heartbeat hammered.

Her mouth parted.

She shouldn't — she really shouldn't — but she tipped her chin up the tiniest bit, drawn in like a moth to fire.

Logan's gaze dropped to her lips.

His jaw flexed like he was fighting himself.

He braced one hand on the wall beside her head, effectively caging her in without touching her.

"Darlin'…" he breathed.

"If you take one more step toward me, I'm not stoppin' this time."

Her hand moved before her mind did — fingers knotting in the front of his jacket.

Logan's inhale was sharp, wrecked. He pressed closer, his body fitting into hers like it was a promise years in the making.

He lowered his forehead to hers, voice dangerously low, a whisper meant to ruin her.

"You keep pullin' me in like that, and I swear, Avery… I'll make you forget your own damn name."

Her whole body trembled. Heat washed through her so fast she stumbled forward into him. His hands caught her waist instantly, like he'd been waiting for the excuse.

"Logan—" she whispered, breathless, helpless.

He bent toward her mouth—

CRUNCH. CRUNCH. CRUNCH.

Boots on snow.

They froze.

Then:

"Avery? Logan? We brought more coffee!"

Both parents.

Together.

Walking straight into the barn.

Avery nearly collapsed on the spot.

Logan's grip tightened at her waist — steadying her while he silently cursed the universe.

He stepped back so slowly it hurt, dragging his fingers along her hip like he didn't want to let go. Under his breath, only for her:

"I'm gonna lose my mind."

Her mom popped through the doorway, carrying a thermos.

"Oh! There you two are! We thought you might want something warm."

Logan straightened immediately, smiling perfectly polite, as if he hadn't just promised Avery she wouldn't remember her own name.

"Perfect timing," he said cheerfully.

Avery shot him a look that said: You're a menace.

Logan only smirked — soft, dark, and entirely unrepentant.

Logan brushed past her, his fingers grazing her waist in a way that felt anything but accidental.

"Later," he murmured, low enough to curl heat straight through her.

He paused in the barn doorway, glancing back just long enough for his eyes to lock with hers — dark, hungry, unshaken by every interruption the day had thrown at them.

"And trust me, Avery…"

His voice dropped to a warning that hit her like a shiver.

"…I won't get interrupted twice."

Avery's breath caught, her pulse stumbling as the words sank into her like a promise she wasn't sure she was ready for — but wanted anyway.

The cold outside didn't stand a chance.

She was burning.

Chapter 16

Tempted By His Touch

Avery woke to the soft light of late morning spilling across the cabin. The snow outside glistened like tiny diamonds, untouched, pristine, and utterly beautiful. Yet, she couldn't focus on the scenery. Logan's presence still lingered in her mind, the memory of their closeness from the night before pressing against her consciousness like a secret she couldn't quite contain.

She dressed quickly, pulling on a warm sweater and boots, though her hands trembled slightly—not from the cold, but from the memory of his hands, his touch, and the way he had held her so intimately. Every glance he'd given her had been charged, teasing, promising. She shook her head, trying to focus. *It's just pretend,* she told herself. But even as she said it, her pulse betrayed her, racing at the thought of his proximity.

Downstairs, she found Logan already awake, standing by the window, hands tucked into the pockets of his worn jacket. The sun glinted off the snow, highlighting the sharp planes of his face, the slight curl of his lips, and the intensity of his dark eyes. Even in casual silence, he seemed to command the room, and her breath hitched.

"Morning," he said, voice low, just enough for her to feel it in her chest.

"Morning," she replied, brushing a strand of hair behind her ear. She wanted to sound casual, but her voice came out soft, betraying her inner turmoil.

Logan turned, leaning against the counter, watching her with a slow, deliberate gaze. "You're… quiet this morning," he said, the smirk tugging at his lips. "Planning your next move, Doc?"

Avery's stomach fluttered. "Maybe I'm just thinking about work," she said, keeping her tone neutral.

"Uh-huh," he murmured, clearly unconvinced. "About work, huh?" He stepped closer, each movement deliberate, slow, and teasing. "Or about me?"

Heat pooled low in her belly, and she couldn't meet his gaze directly. "I—" She paused, trying to form a sentence that didn't sound like surrender. "I have patients to think about."

"Patients," he echoed, drawing out the word. "Right. But you were thinking about me last night, weren't you?"

Her cheeks flushed hot, and she looked away, fiddling with the hem of her sweater. "Maybe," she whispered, and even that sounded dangerously vulnerable.

He smiled, slow and predatory, as he stepped closer, the warmth of him brushing against her in a way that felt intentional. "You know," he murmured, voice low and teasing, "mornings like this are trouble. Snow… quiet… and you looking at me like that."

Avery swallowed hard, every nerve tuned to the subtle flex of his shoulders, the heat in his eyes. She'd worked beside him on this ranch plenty of times — fixed fences with him, fed animals with him — but somehow this morning felt different. Charged. Heated. Dangerous.

Logan noticed.

Of course he did.

"Come on," he said suddenly, nudging her shoulder with his. "Let's take a walk."

She blinked. "A walk? We've already been everywhere out here."

"Yeah," he said, lips curving, "but you've been workin' every time. Today… I want you to see it. Really see it. The way I do."

Her breath hitched — not because of the ranch, but because of the way he said the way I do, like there was something important, something intimate he'd been waiting to show her.

"Alright," she whispered.

They pulled on their coats and stepped outside. Snow crunched under their boots, the world washed in soft silver light. Logan adjusted the cuff of her sleeve — a simple gesture, but his fingers lingered just long enough to make her heart stutter.

"You okay?" he asked quietly, like he didn't already know the answer.

"I'm fine," she lied breathlessly.

His smirk was sinful. "Sure you are."

And then he led her out into the snow—still pretending to be married, still telling themselves none of this meant anything… while both of them felt everything anyway.

They ventured from barn to pasture, Logan pointing out details she had never noticed—the way sunlight caught the frost on the fence posts, the tracks of deer through the snow, the quiet artistry of the frozen pond. Avery found herself watching him as much as she watched the landscape, marveling at the ease of his movements, the quiet strength he exuded, the way he made even mundane work look almost hypnotic.

"You see what I mean?" he asked, voice softening as they paused on a ridge overlooking the ranch. "All of this… it's alive. You just have to know how to look."

Avery nodded, heart thudding. "I see it," she said, but the words weren't just about the ranch. They were about him, too. The way he moved, the way he looked at her, the tension coiling in the air between them.

He stepped closer, reducing the distance until their shoulders brushed. "You know," he murmured, voice dropping, "every time I see you like this… I can't decide whether to keep teasing you or finally… show you how much I want you."

Her pulse quickened, breath hitching. "Logan—" she started, voice trembling.

"Shh," he said softly, pressing a finger to her lips. His other hand brushed lightly down her arm, lingering, testing, igniting sparks at every touch. "No talking. Just… feel."

Avery's knees went weak, the snow around her forgotten, the world narrowing to the heat of him, the tease of his touch, and the delicious tension she had fought so hard to ignore.

Logan pushed her up against the wooden post of the fence. Caging her in with his body. He gazed into her eyes longingly and then he claimed her lips as if he was claiming her world for himself. The kiss was soft and tender at first. Logan having all the control. He moved from her lips placing soft tender kisses on her neck by the spot right behind her ear. Knowing that, that spot drove her wild he continued to kiss there and teased her a little. Slowly moving to her collarbone and sucking on her flesh til it glowed red with his marks. Avery got desperate. She couldn't take it anymore. She needed his lips on hers. She pulled him back up to her mouth and kissed him hard and demandingly. They both fought for dominance as their kiss deepened as if the world had just disappeared and it was just them.

When they finally pulled back, breaths shallow and hearts racing, Avery leaned against him, grounding herself in the sensation of warmth, trust, and unspoken desire. Logan's arms wrapped around her, holding her close yet giving her just enough space to maintain her composure.

They wandered back to the cabin, hands brushing, shoulders occasionally pressing together, each contact electric. Avery couldn't stop stealing glances at him, reading every dark smirk, every playful tilt of his lips, every teasing arch of his brow.

Once inside, the heat between them didn't cool. He hovered near the kitchen, pretending to pour cocoa while his gaze never left hers. Every movement was deliberate, slow, and calculated to keep her on edge.

"You know," he said quietly, leaning closer under the guise of adjusting the blanket on the couch, "I can't decide if I like teasing you or… actually seeing how much you want me."

Avery shivered despite the warmth of the fire, breath catching. "You're impossible," she whispered, but the heat in her voice betrayed her desire.

"And yet," he murmured, voice dropping, "you haven't walked away. Haven't told me you want to leave. Which tells me… you're thinking about me as much as I'm thinking about you."

The tension coiled tighter between them, magnetic and inescapable. Avery's fingers lingered near his, subtle touches sparking a fire she couldn't ignore.

Even in casual conversation—fetching cocoa, adjusting the blanket, brushing past him to pour cream—every motion was charged, every glance heavy with anticipation.

Avery realized, with a mixture of fear and exhilaration, that the line between pretend and real desire had blurred entirely. Every teasing word, every lingering touch, every playful smirk was a countdown to a moment she both feared and craved.

By the time evening fell, the cabin seemed smaller, the world outside muffled by the storm and snow. Logan's gaze lingered on her in ways that left her pulse racing, fingers brushing just long enough to make her shiver, lips curving into a smirk that promised nothing and everything at once.

"You're mine," he murmured, stepping closer. "Even when we pretend. Even when we try to fight it."

Avery swallowed, heart thudding, knowing she couldn't—and didn't want to—fight it anymore.

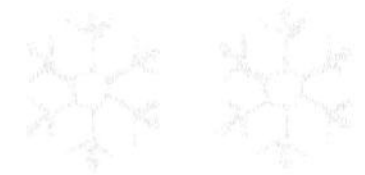

Logan's POV

Logan had been awake long before Avery's footsteps reached the bottom of the stairs.

He'd stood there by the window, hands in his jacket pockets, staring out at the sunlit snow while replaying every second of the night before.

The warmth of her breath against his skin.

The way she whispered his name like it meant something.

The look in her eyes when she finally let herself want him.

He didn't do slow burn.

He didn't do fragile.

But with her?

He couldn't move too fast even if he tried.

He heard her before he saw her—light steps, a soft exhale, the faint rustle of her sweater sleeves—and his pulse tightened. That woman had no idea what she did to him. None.

When she reached the bottom of the stairs, looking small and unsure and devastatingly beautiful, he had to bite the inside of his cheek to keep from pulling her into his arms again.

"Morning," he said, voice lower than he meant. It always dropped around her.

She whispered it back, soft as snowfall.

He watched her carefully, noting the tremble in her hands. Not fear—want.

And damn, if that didn't go straight to his chest.

Avery tried to play casual, talking about work, patients, anything to avoid admitting what they both felt simmering under the surface.

He stepped closer, letting the warmth of his body brush hers.

"About work, huh?" he murmured.

Her eyes darted away. Her breath hitched.

He smirked.

Yeah. He wasn't imagining it.

He'd wanted to kiss her right there in the kitchen—and he almost did—but something stopped him. She wasn't ready yet. Not fully. And he needed her to want him without the storm, without the pretending, without the pressure.

So he offered a walk.

Neutral. Harmless. Safe.

Except it wasn't.

The minute they stepped outside, the cold hit him but the warmth of her beside him did more damage than the snow ever could. She kept brushing against him without realizing it—her sleeve, her hand, the small bump of her hip—and every small touch sent heat through him like wildfire.

He shouldn't want her this much.

He knew it.

Didn't matter.

Up on the ridge, with the whole ranch stretched behind them and sunlight catching in her curls, something in his chest shifted. She wasn't just beautiful. She was alive in a way he hadn't realized he was craving.

She looked at the frozen pond.

He looked at her.

When she turned back toward him, eyes soft and uncertain, he stepped closer almost without thinking.

Every warning bell in his mind went off.

Too close.

Too fast.

Too much.

But she didn't back away.

"Every time I see you like this…" he said softly, letting the truth slip through, "I can't decide whether to keep teasing you or finally show you how much I want you."

Her breath caught—a tiny, desperate sound.

His restraint snapped.

He touched her first—light, just a brush of his fingers down her arm—but she leaned into it like her body already belonged to him.

And that was it.

Fence post, cold air, her flushed cheeks, his hands sliding up her waist—

He kissed her because he couldn't not kiss her.

Slow.

Claiming.

Gentle enough to check if she'd pull away, hard enough to tell her he wasn't pretending anymore.

She kissed him back like she'd been starving for it.

Every sound she made—the soft gasp when he kissed her neck, the small whimper when he sucked gently at her skin—settled deep in his chest, claiming space he hadn't meant to give up.

When she yanked him back to her mouth, he let her take control—just for a second—because seeing Avery desperate for him was something he'd replay for the rest of his damn life.

He didn't realize how far he'd fallen until they stopped, breathless, her forehead resting against his, her hands still fisted in his jacket.

He kept his voice gentle. "Get some air," he whispered, though he was the one who needed it.

Walking back to the cabin, he kept stealing glances at her—her flushed cheeks, her swollen lips, the way she kept touching her fingers like she could still feel him there.

Inside, the fire popped.

Avery hovered near the couch, trying to calm her pulse.

Logan leaned against the counter, pretending to fix cocoa while watching her with every bit of hunger he tried and failed to hide.

He wanted her again.

Wanted to kiss her until the line between pretending and reality didn't exist.

He almost said the words he wasn't supposed to say.

You're mine.

But instead, he stepped closer, letting his voice go low, rough—honest.

"You're thinking about me," he murmured.

A blush rose on her chest. Visible. Beautiful.

"And I'm thinking about you."

Her breath wavered.

"And that's a problem," he said.

Because it was.

Because it wasn't supposed to feel this real.

When she whispered that she didn't want him to stop, that was the moment he knew—

He wasn't playing pretend anymore.

He scooped her chin with his fingers, gave her one slow look that said everything he couldn't say out loud.

"You're mine," he murmured, almost to himself.

But she heard it.

And she didn't pull away.

Chapter 17

Jealously Burns

The storm had passed, but the air between them hadn't softened. It felt charged—alive with all the things they hadn't said since that night tangled in the dark.

Avery stretched under the sheets, muscles tender and slow to wake. When she finally opened her eyes, Logan was already up, standing by the window, coffee in hand, staring out over the snow-dusted pasture.

"Morning," she murmured, voice still rough from sleep.

He turned slightly, his lips twitching. "Morning, wife."

The word wife hit her harder than it should have. Pretend or not, it sounded different now—warmer, heavier, dangerously close to feeling real.

They moved through breakfast quietly. Every brush of fingers, every sidelong glance hummed with something unsaid.

By early evening, Avery stood in front of the mirror, smoothing down her dress for the winter festival in town.

She hadn't dressed up in weeks. Maybe that's why she wanted to—maybe she wanted to feel like more than the snowbound "fake wife" on the ranch.

The fitted emerald dress hit just above her knees, soft fabric catching the firelight. The skirt swayed when she moved, brushing against the tops of her tan cowboy boots. A gold necklace glinted at her collarbone, and her honey-brown curls framed her face in soft, natural waves.

When she turned, she caught sight of Logan's reflection in the doorway.

His hand froze halfway through buttoning his flannel.

"You sure you wanna wear that, Doc?" he asked finally, his voice quiet but rough.

Avery arched an eyebrow. "What's wrong with it?"

He stepped closer, slow and deliberate, his eyes dragging down her body with open appreciation that made her skin prickle. "Nothin's wrong with it. Except every man in that bar's gonna forget his drink when you walk in."

"It's a dress, Logan. People wear them."

"Yeah," he muttered, jaw tightening. "Just not my wife."

She laughed softly, brushing past him to grab her coat. "Pretend wife, remember?"

He didn't answer right away. Just watched her leave, a muscle ticking in his jaw.

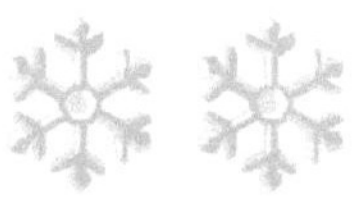

The winter festival glowed against the falling snow, a swirl of warm lights and cold air. Families wandered between wooden stalls strung with garland, sipping steaming cocoa as carolers sang beside a crackling firepit. Kids tossed snowballs near the ice-sculpture display, their laughter echoing across the square. The scent of roasted chestnuts drifted through the air, mingling with the crisp bite of winter pine and distant hints of mulled wine.

Couples danced beneath the lanterns, boots scuffing across the snow-dusted ground as a fiddle played from a makeshift stage. Strings of lights wrapped around every pole and rooftop, giving the whole town a soft golden glow that made even strangers smile at one another.

It was small-town Christmas magic in its purest form.

The kind that wrapped itself around you, warm and impossible to shake.

And somewhere among the music and snow and holiday chaos…

The winter festival had spilled into the local tavern—music, laughter, and the smell of whiskey warming the air. Avery had been pulled into conversation with one of the rodeo sponsors, a charming man with an easy grin and a little too much liquid courage.

Logan arrived late. The moment his boots hit the floorboards, his gaze found her.

And froze.

Avery stood by the counter, laughing politely, her curls tumbling over her shoulder as the man leaned in closer. Logan could see it all—the way the guy's hand brushed her arm, the way Avery smiled awkwardly, trying to be polite.

Then it happened.

The man dipped his head and kissed her—on the lips.

Not an accident. Not a joke.

A real kiss.

Avery shoved him back, startled. "What the hell—"

But before she could finish, Logan was already moving.

The bar seemed to still around him, like everyone could feel the danger before it hit. He crossed the room in three long strides, grabbed the man by the collar, and slammed him against the wall hard enough to rattle the glasses on the shelf.

"You touch my wife again," Logan growled, voice low and dark, "and you're gonna be eatin' through a straw."

The man sputtered, hands raised. "Whoa—hey, I didn't know she was—"

"Didn't know?" Logan's fist tightened. "You saw the ring."

"Logan!" Avery's voice cut through the noise. "Stop!"

He didn't. His chest heaved, eyes burning into the man's face. "Say her name again," he hissed. "Go on. See what happens."

The guy shoved back, trying to look tough. "What, you gonna fight me over some fake—"

That was it. Logan swung.

The sound of the punch cracked through the bar. The man hit the ground hard, a chair tipping over with him. Someone gasped; someone else yelled, "Hey, hey, break it up!"

Avery grabbed Logan's arm, heart pounding. "Logan, stop it! Let's go!"

He stood over the man for a beat longer, breathing hard, every muscle tense like he was still deciding whether to throw another punch. Then he let Avery pull him toward the door.

The entire bar watched them leave in silence.

Snow crunched beneath their boots, the icy air stinging her cheeks. Avery spun on him as soon as they reached the truck.

"What was that?!"

He turned, eyes still blazing. "That was me watching some drunk idiot put his hands on my wife!"

"Pretend wife!" she shot back. "You can't go around punching people just because—"

"Just because what?" he snapped, voice low, raw. "Because I care? Because seeing another man kiss you makes me want to break something?"

Her breath caught. "You're insane."

"Yeah," he said roughly, taking a step closer. "Only when it comes to you."

The snow fell harder, cold flakes clinging to his hair. His anger was still there—hot and alive—but underneath it was something she couldn't name. Something that made her chest ache.

"You can't keep acting like this," she whispered. "We're supposed to be pretending, Logan. This—whatever this is—it's not part of the deal."

He laughed bitterly and low. "You think I can just flip that off? You think I can watch another man touch you and not feel like I'm gonna come apart?"

She looked up at him; her pulse racing. "It was a mistake. He kissed me before I could stop him."

"I don't care if it was a mistake," he said, voice rough with something dangerously close to pain. "He still touched what's mine."

Avery's breath hitched. "You don't own me."

He met her gaze, eyes dark and unguarded. "No. But I damn sure love you like I do."

Her heart stopped.

The words hung in the cold night air, shocking them both into silence.

He stepped back a fraction, jaw tight. "Guess that ruined the whole pretend part, huh?"

Before she could answer, he turned away, climbing into the truck. Avery stood there for a long moment, snow collecting in her hair, her pulse still trembling with everything that had just been said—and everything that hadn't.

Back at the cabin, the silence was louder than the wind outside. Logan sat by the fire, his knuckles scraped, his expression unreadable.

Avery stood at the edge of the room, arms crossed. "You can't do that again," she whispered. "You can't just throw punches every time someone looks at me wrong."

His eyes lifted to hers, tired but fierce. "Then stop looking at them like that."

She blinked. "Like what?"

"Like you don't know what you do to me."

The words were soft, dangerous.

For a moment, neither moved. Then, Avery crossed the room slowly, her voice low. "You don't get to say things like that and then act like it means nothing."

He looked up at her, the corner of his mouth curving into something small and broken. "Who said it doesn't?"

The space between them vanished.

This time, when he kissed her, it wasn't out of anger—it was desperation, heat, apology, and something far too real for either of them to keep pretending.

Avery should've pushed him away. She should have told him it was all pretend, and their relationship was not supposed to survive after the Christmas season.

But when his hands cupped her face, when his thumb brushed the corner of her mouth like he was afraid she might break, every reason to stop dissolved.

The kiss deepened—slow, aching, desperate. He kissed her like a man starved for truth, and she answered him like she'd been waiting her whole life to be found.

Her fingers slid into his hair, still cold from the night air, and he breathed her name like it was both a confession and a prayer.

"You scare me," she whispered against his lips, her voice trembling.

He rested his forehead against hers, chest rising and falling fast. "Good," he murmured. "'Cause you terrify me too."

They stood there for a long moment; the firelight flickering over them, painting his bruised jaw in gold. His hand traced the curve of her neck, sliding to her shoulder, gentle where his temper had been anything but.

"I didn't mean to lose it," he said finally, voice rough. "But when I saw him touch you… I saw red. I just—couldn't stand it."

Avery swallowed hard. "You can't keep protecting me like that, Logan. Not from everyone. Not from everything."

He nodded once, his thumb brushing her collarbone. "Maybe not. But I can damn sure try."

Her laugh was soft, shaky. "You're impossible."

His lips curved into something small and unguarded. "And you love that about me."

She didn't deny it. Couldn't.

Because when he looked at her that way—like she was both his undoing and his only peace—her heart forgot every line they'd drawn.

He reached for her hand, threading his fingers through hers. "Come here," he whispered, voice low and steady.

She let him pull her closer until the air between them was nothing but heat and heartbeats.

The tension that had burned through the night finally broke—melting into something quieter, sweeter, more dangerous.

Avery's breath caught when his thumb brushed the side of her neck, tracing the flutter of her pulse. The world seemed to narrow to the rhythm of their breathing, the quiet crackle of the fire, the warmth rolling off his skin.

He tilted her chin up, his gaze flicking from her eyes to her mouth and back again. "You sure you want this?" he asked softly, his voice a rasp—part restraint, part reverence.

She nodded, heart pounding. "I've never been surer of anything."

That was all it took.

Logan's hand slid to her waist, pulling her against him with a care that contradicted every ounce of his roughness. Their lips met again, slower this time—less battle, more surrender. The kind of kiss that stripped everything else away until only truth remained.

Her hands found the edge of his shirt, fingers brushing against warm skin, the steady beat of his heart under her palm. He drew in a sharp breath, resting his forehead against hers, like he needed that small touch to anchor himself.

"I don't deserve you," he murmured.

Avery's lips curved faintly. "Good thing you don't get to decide that."

He laughed softly, the sound low and unsteady. "You drive me crazy, you know that?"

"I'm aware," she whispered, her breath ghosting across his lips. "Now shut up and kiss me again."

The next kiss wasn't soft—it was hungry, full of all the words they hadn't said, all the feelings they'd spent weeks pretending not to have. His fingers tangled in her curls; her hands traced the lines of his shoulders, memorizing the strength and the warmth beneath them.

When they finally broke apart, both were breathless. He rested his forehead against hers once more, whispering, "If this is pretend, I never want it to end."

She smiled, small and genuine. "Then maybe we stop pretending."

Outside, snow drifted quietly past the window, the night still and silver. Inside, the firelight danced over them, soft and golden, as the distance between them disappeared for good.

Chapter 18

Confessions and Cravings

The morning sun had barely crested the horizon when Avery stirred. Warmth pressed against her back—steady, strong, dangerously familiar. Logan's arm rested heavy across her waist, their legs tangled in sheets that still carried the heat of last night's storm.

Her breath caught.

Everything felt… different.

Softer.

Sharper.

Too real to pretend.

Logan shifted behind her, letting out a low morning hum that vibrated through her spine.

"Morning," he murmured, voice still gravel-soft from sleep.

She turned slightly. "Morning."

A slow, sleepy smirk curved his lips. "Sleep alright, wife?"

The word landed warm and dangerous, curling low in her stomach.

Pretend wife.

Actual effect.

They moved through breakfast with a new rhythm—gentler, more deliberate. Every brush of his hand sent sparks down her spine. Every glance held something deeper, something like a promise he wasn't ready to speak out loud.

By mid-morning, Avery needed space. The cabin felt too full of last night—too full of him. She grabbed her bag, mumbling something about checking on the mobile clinic.

Logan insisted on driving.

"I wanna see what you do," he said, leaning against the truck with that infuriating, irresistible confidence. "The part of you nobody else gets to see."

Her heart nearly tripped over itself, but she didn't argue.

At the community center, Avery stepped into her element—steady, focused, quietly fierce. She moved from patient to patient with a calm, practiced certainty. Logan watched from the doorway, arms crossed, eyes following her like he was memorizing every breath she took.

During a quiet moment, she slipped outside to cool off. Logan followed, boots crunching in the snow.

"You're incredible," he whispered.

Avery blinked. "I was just doing my job."

"Not the way you do it." His gaze warmed. "My papaw used to say you can tell a good soul by how they treat folks who can't give 'em nothin' back."

Her breath caught.

Logan stepped closer, gently brushing a curl from her cheek.

"Watchin' you today… he'd have liked you, Doc."

A beat.

"He'd have liked you a whole lot."

Her heart squeezed—shock, longing, and something she didn't want to name.

"Logan…"

He shook his head, eyes darkening. "Don't look at me like that unless you want me kissin' you right here in front of half the damn town."

Her breath stuttered.

She definitely wanted that.

But she also definitely wasn't ready.

So she smiled—soft, shy, undone.

"Come on. We still have work to do."

That night, the weight of the day followed them back to the cabin. The fire crackled, wind rattling the windows as winter pressed close around them.

Logan leaned against the counter, watching her move around the kitchen with a quiet intensity that made every hair on her neck rise.

"You were somethin' today," he murmured.

"You already said that," she said, flustered.

"Didn't say enough."

He crossed the distance slowly—like a man approaching something sacred.

"You keep hidin'," he whispered, brushing her wrist with his thumb. "But I see you."

Her pulse fluttered under his touch.

"You don't know everything," she breathed.

"Know enough." His gaze softened. "Know how you forget to take care of yourself but never forget anyone else."

His hand lifted to her jaw, gentle as snowfall.

"And how you think you gotta earn love when you already deserve it."

Her breath trembled.

The air thickened—soft and molten.

"I don't quit easily," she whispered.

"I know." His voice roughened. "I saw it today—those people lookin' at you like you hung the damn moon."

She froze.

He'd noticed that?

He'd noticed everything?

"Don't ever shrink yourself," he said. "You give this town somethin' it didn't know it needed."

His thumb swept her pulse again.

"And you give me somethin' I didn't know I needed."

Avery stepped closer before she could stop herself.

"Logan… what are we doing?"

"Somethin' stupid," he murmured. "Somethin' dangerous."

"Then why can't we stop?"

A soft, broken laugh left him.

"Because you terrify me."

Her heart twisted. "You scare me too."

"Good."

The word pulled her in.

Then, his hands slid to her waist.

Her fingers curled into his shirt.

And the space between them disappeared entirely.

He kissed her slowly.

Deep.

Not like last night's storm.

But like something he'd been afraid of wanting.

Something real.

His forehead rested against hers.

"If this is pretend," he whispered, "I never want it to end."

She breathed against his mouth.

"Then maybe we stop pretending."

He exhaled—shaky, relieved, wanting.

His hand slid along her back, drawing her closer…

…and the rest of the night unfolded in soft firelight and quiet closeness, the world beyond the cabin fading into nothing.

Wrapped in his arms beneath the quilt, Avery whispered the words she didn't mean to say out loud:

"Maybe I need someone who sees me."

Logan kissed the top of her head, voice barely a breath.

"Nah, sweetheart…"

He pulled her closer—slow, protective, sure.

"You need a person who truly understands you."

Chapter 19

Trapped Together, Heartbeats Collide

The wind had picked up again by late afternoon, snow swirling so thick it nearly erased the edges of the cabin from view. Avery stood at the window, watching as the world outside vanished behind white sheets of winter. The storm wasn't just back—it was furious, determined; it was the kind of storm that made roads disappear and silence settle heavy.

Logan was still out in the barn when she checked last, stacking hay bales with the fluid precision she'd come to admire. She'd offered to help—of course she had—but he insisted she stay inside where it was warm.

Now, with flurries thick enough to blur the world, she realized what that really meant.

They were stuck.

Together.

Alone.

The word alone carried a weight that settled right in her chest. A warm, terrifying weight.

Logan pushed the door open a moment later, brushing snow from his jacket, the cold air clinging to the scent of cedar and leather that always followed him in.

"Looks like we're not goin' anywhere for a while," he said, voice low, teasing—but with an undercurrent that made her pulse jump.

Avery let out a breathy laugh, tugging at the hem of her sweater. "You don't say. I guess we're stuck here together."

"Stuck," he repeated, his gaze meeting hers. His mouth curved into a slow, knowing smirk. "Sounds like it could be perilous."

"Perilous?" she repeated, heartbeat already thundering.

"Yes." He took a step closer. Then another. "Being this close… with nowhere to run. Forced to notice things you shouldn't. Feel things you ain't ready to admit."

His shoulder brushed hers. Barely. Teasing. A whisper of contact that sent a spark straight through her ribcage.

The cabin felt smaller when they stepped back inside—like the walls had moved in, like the fire's glow had sharpened every shadow. The storm outside formed a cocoon, isolating them from the world, amplifying the tension in every glance.

"Want some cocoa?" She asked, her voice lighter than she felt.

"I think I'd rather watch you."

Logan leaned against the doorway, arms crossed, gaze so direct it burned. "See how you move. How you think? How you… everything."

Her breath wobbled. Her hands trembled as she made the cocoa, every flick of his gaze setting her nerves alight. He wasn't flirting—he was studying her. Inviting her to be seen.

They sat near the fire, mugs in hand, silence stretching long enough to feel dangerous. Avery felt his attention like a touch low on her spine.

"I can't believe the storm," she murmured, tracing the rim of her mug.

"Believe it," he said, leaning closer. The heat from his body brushed her arm. "Or… we could stop pretendin' we're safe and see what happens."

Her pulse stuttered. "Logan…"

"Say my name again," he murmured. Low. Intimate. A command wrapped in velvet.

Avery shivered.

"Logan."

His smile was slow. Predatory. Soft.

"Good. That's a start."

The storm raged on, wind howling against the windows, but inside, the only thing she could feel was him. His knee brushed against hers. The way his fingers "accidentally" grazed her hand. Her body was a live wire—every touch sparking something she couldn't control.

Logan cupped her waist and pulled her closer, the movement slow and certain, like he'd been holding himself back for far too long. Avery barely had time to breathe before his mouth found hers—hungry, searching, but reverent in a way that made her knees buckle.

She slid into his lap without thinking; her legs straddling him as his hands settled at her hips, grounding her, guiding her. Part of her whispered she didn't deserve this—didn't deserve him—but the way he held her made her want to believe she did.

Their breaths tangled, kisses growing deeper, more desperate. Logan kissed like a man trying to memorize her, like he didn't know where to touch her first because he wanted to touch her everywhere.

His hands slid beneath her sweater, warm and sure against her skin. Avery gasped, fingers gripping his shoulders, feeling every line of strength beneath her palms.

"Sweetheart," he breathed, voice breaking a little, "if you keep makin' those sounds, I'm not gonna last another damn second bein' gentle."

Her answer was a soft, involuntary sound—one that had his breath shuddering.

He eased her down onto the rug beside the fire, covering her with his body as he kissed along her jaw, down her throat, slow and teasing, like he was savoring the taste of every new inch of her. The fire crackled beside them; the storm roared outside, but all Avery felt was heat.

Logan's hand slid along her side, his lips returning to hers in a kiss that left her trembling.

Everything else disappeared.

Hours blurred into teasing touches and whispered confessions. Avery found herself leaning closer without meaning to, letting the warmth of him seep into her bones.

Logan stood at one point, stretching, shirt tugging tight across his chest. Avery's gaze lingered—helpless, hungry. Logan noticed. God, he noticed.

"You know," he said, stepping closer, voice a low rumble, "I could get used to havin' you this close. Every damn night."

Avery swallowed, trying—failing—to hide her reaction. "Every night? You're not very subtle, you know."

"Subtlety doesn't suit me." His smirk deepened. "Neither does waitin' when I want somethin'… or someone."

Her heart thudded hard enough to hurt.

They ended up back on the rug near the fire, closer than before—knees brushing, fingers brushing, until his hand found hers again… and didn't leave.

The air between them grew taut, heavy with unspoken invitation. Desire coiled through her, thick and urgent.

Avery's soft moan filled the space between them as Logan's mouth trailed down her neck, lingering at the spot that made her arch into him. His hands moved with slow confidence, mapping the shape of her waist, her hips, the gentle curve of her body like he'd dreamed about it.

She guided him back to her with a needy tug of his shirt, and he followed willingly—almost desperately—pressing a line of gentle kisses along her shoulder before returning to her lips.

"Look at me," he whispered.

She did.

And the hunger in his eyes nearly unraveled her.

"You feel incredible," he murmured, thumb brushing the inside of her arm, sending a shock of warmth through her. "Been tryin' to be patient… but every time you touch me…" He shook his head slightly, breath unsteady. "You undo me."

The firelight flickered across his face, turning the moment molten. Outside, the storm clawed at the cabin walls, but the real lightning was in the way he looked at her.

The world outside was howling, but inside, the only sound was their uneven breaths and the quiet, intimate sighs that slipped from Avery's lips as Logan kissed her again—deeper this time, slower, like he wanted this memory burned into both of them.

His fingers intertwined with hers, squeezing gently, grounding her as their bodies pressed closer, heat rising between them until she wasn't sure where she ended and he began.

The storm outside had nothing on them.

By midnight, the cabin felt like another world—one made of warmth and firelight and breathless closeness. Every touch felt deliberate. Every glance a question. Every exhale a confession neither of them said out loud.

Logan leaned in, forehead resting against hers, breath warm against her cheek.

"Avery…" His voice was rough, intimate, unraveling. "I don't wanna pretend anymore. I can't."

Her heart flipped.

"Neither can I," she whispered, voice trembling.

The fire had burned low, embers glowing like scattered stars, but inside, the world had narrowed to the beat of their hearts—colliding, syncing, surrendering.

Avery rested against his chest, breath still unsteady, her skin warm from everything they'd shared. Logan held her close, his hand tracing slow, absentminded circles on her back, like he couldn't stop touching her even if he tried.

She listened to the steady rhythm of his heartbeat beneath her cheek—a calm, grounding thump that made her chest ache in a way she wasn't ready to examine. Logan dipped his head, brushing a soft kiss to her temple.

"Hey," he murmured softly, voice still rough around the edges. "Look at me."

She lifted her gaze, unsure of what she'd find in his eyes.

What she saw nearly undid her.

There was heat, yes—but also something deeper. Something unguarded.

"There's nothin' pretend about this," he whispered. "Not anymore."

Avery swallowed hard, emotion rising in her throat. She curled closer to him, unable to hide how much those words shook her.

Logan tightened his arm around her, pulling her even closer under the quilt.

His breath warmed the top of her head as he whispered,

"Not one damn thing."

By the time the night surrendered to quiet, Avery knew the truth as surely as she knew her own name: the storm hadn't just trapped them. It had revealed them.

And as she drifted toward sleep with Logan's arm wrapped around her, their shared heat lingering on her skin, she felt something undeniable settle deep in her chest.

This wasn't temptation anymore.

It was inevitable.

Chapter 20

Falling Hard, Wanting More

The storm lingered for days, turning the ranch into a quiet island of white. The fences disappeared beneath drifts, the barn roof glittered with frost, and the world seemed to slow to the rhythm of the fire crackling in Logan's cabin.

Avery had stopped counting how long it had been since she'd left the property. It didn't feel like being stuck anymore. It felt like being suspended—between the life she thought she knew and whatever this was becoming.

She stood at the window that morning, a coffee mug warming her hands, watching the horse's nose through the snow near the fence. Logan's flannel hung loosely off her shoulders; she hadn't even realized she'd slipped it on again until she caught her reflection in the glass.

It smelled like him—cedar, smoke, and a hint of something darker she could never name.

"Planning on going to work dressed like that?" Logan's voice drifted from behind her, lazy and teasing.

She turned, pretending to scowl. "I told you. I'm off for the holidays. But I could absolutely pull this off at the hospital."

He grinned from the kitchen, flipping pancakes with ridiculous ease. "Not unless you want every male nurse walkin' into walls."

A blush crept up her neck. "Is this normal for you? Flirting first thing in the morning?"

"Only when you're in my shirt," he said lightly, "and you look too pretty for me to pretend I'm not."

Her breath caught. She tried to roll her eyes, but failed. "You're being ridiculous."

"And you're still eating my food," he said as he set the plate in front of her.

Avery's smile bloomed. "Maybe I like the cook."

"Guess it's working."

It was dangerously easy, the rhythm they'd fallen into—teasing breakfasts, stolen glances, quiet moments where their knees brushed without either of them pulling away. The fake husband act had dissolved somewhere along the way, replaced by something heavier. Something neither could name yet.

After breakfast, Logan tugged on his coat. "Alright, doctor. Let's see if you can still handle ranch work after keepin' me up half the night with your talkin'."

Avery scoffed. "Please. I've mucked stalls, fed horses, fixed fences—"

"And yet…" He smirked. "I still think you've got more to prove."

She stepped closer. "Oh? Is that a challenge?"

"Sweetheart, it's always a challenge with you."

The wind bit at her cheeks as they trudged to the barn. Inside, the air was warmer, rich with hay and the familiar scent of horses. Avery inhaled deeply—it was strangely grounding.

Logan showed her how to check the feed, fix a latch, and brush a horse's coat until it gleamed. His sleeves were rolled up, forearms dusted with sawdust, movements strong but easy.

She tried to focus. She truly did.

But she found herself watching him instead.

"You're staring," he said without looking up.

"I am not."

"You are." He glanced over his shoulder with a slow, devastating smile. "I can feel it."

"Maybe I'm just impressed."

He stepped closer, passing her the brush. His hand grazed hers—warm, deliberate. "Then I'll take that as a compliment, Doc."

Her heart skipped. "You enjoy making me flustered."

"Maybe." He leaned in. "Or maybe I just like seeing you look at me like that."

She swallowed. "Like what?"

"Like you're tryin' not to want me."

Her breath hitched. "Logan—"

He stepped back, his smirk softening. "Relax, Avery. Teasin'."

Except it wasn't really teasing. They both felt the current sparking every time they got too close.

They worked in silence for a while, but the air was charged. When he handed her a shovel, their fingers brushed again—and neither looked away.

By afternoon, the sky had darkened again. Snow fell in soft, thick sheets. Logan lit lanterns in the barn, the glow turning the wooden walls warm and golden.

"You were right," she admitted. "This is harder than it looks."

"Told you. But you did good."

"Coming from you," she teased, "I'll take that as high praise."

He chuckled. "You learn quickly."

Warmth bloomed in her chest. "You sound surprised."

"Not surprised." His voice softened, losing its teasing edge. "Just… proud."

Her breath hitched—sharp, involuntary. "Logan… don't."

He lifted his brows. "Don't what?"

Avery looked away, brushing her glove over the mare's back as if focusing on the animal might steady her pulse. It didn't. "Don't say things that make this harder than it already is."

"Harder how?" His steps were slow, deliberate, boot scuffing softly against the hay-covered floor as he closed the distance between them. "We're supposed to be good at pretending."

"That's the problem," she whispered. "You make pretend feel real."

Logan stopped just inches from her, close enough that she felt the heat radiating off him in waves.

"Or," he murmured, voice deepening, "maybe it feels real because it is."

Avery's heart stumbled. "Logan…"

He wasn't smirking now. His gaze had shifted—intense, searching, almost tender in a way that made her stomach drop.

"Avery," he said quietly, "look at me."

She did.
Slowly.
Regretfully.
Helplessly.

The moment her eyes met his, the air tightened like a wire pulled too far. Logan exhaled a breath he'd been holding.

"You keep saying this isn't real," he said softly, "but every time you look at me… every time you touch me… every time I get you to smile when you don't want to? It feels real as hell to me."

Her chest rose with a shaky inhale. "You can't—"

"Yes I can." He moved even closer, his breath warming her cheek. "And I will. Because I'm done pretendin' I don't want you."

The world shrank to the warmth of his body, the quiet of the barn, the faint rhythm of the animals settling around them. Avery's pulse hammered in her throat. She couldn't breathe. Couldn't think.
Could only feel.

"Logan," she whispered—half-warning, half-plea.

He dipped his head, not quite touching her, but close enough that she felt his breath on her lips. "You tell me to back off… really tell me… and I will."

She didn't.
 She couldn't.

Her silence was a truth neither of them were ready to name.

A sudden gust of wind slammed against the barn doors, rattling them on their hinges and shattering the spell between them.

Logan exhaled, long and controlled. He blinked once, like he was pulling himself back into his body.

"Come on," he said gently, his voice rough at the edges. "Let's get inside before the storm traps us again."

He stepped back—reluctantly, slowly—letting the space between them stretch open again like a wound.

Avery could only nod, breath trembling, her heart pounding far too hard for something that was supposed to be pretend.

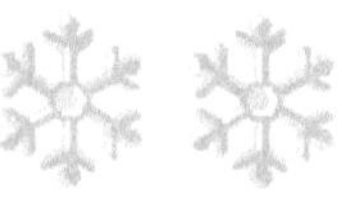

The cabin glowed with firelight when they returned. Avery stood near the hearth, rubbing warmth back into her hands. Logan moved behind her, silent, draping a blanket over her shoulders. His hands lingered—too long, too gentle.

She turned. "You don't have to—"

"I know." His voice dropped. "I want to."

Something inside her wavered. She should've stepped away. Instead, she stayed.

"Logan… what are we doing?"

He looked at her like the answer was written in the air between them. "Whatever this is… it feels right. Doesn't it?"

"It can't just feel right," she whispered. "It has to make sense."

"Doesn't it?" he asked softly.

She didn't answer. Couldn't. The way his thumb brushed her jaw made sense in a way her logic never could.

A breath escaped her—shaky, unsteady.

His hand rose again, thumb catching a tear she hadn't realized had fallen.

"Avery," he murmured, voice trembling at the edges, "if you don't want this… tell me now."

She stepped into him, her voice raw. "I want you."

Logan's breath hitched—quiet, wrecked—before he cupped her face and kissed her. Slow at first, then deeper, warmer, every second unraveling another piece of restraint he'd been clinging to.

Avery clutched the front of his shirt, pulling him closer. His hands slid down to her waist, guiding her gently toward the couch until her knees brushed against it.

He lifted his lips from hers just long enough to breathe, "Sweetheart… you're gonna ruin me."

Her answer was a trembling whisper. "Logan…"

He kissed her again, more urgently this time, like he'd been starving for her and finally let himself taste. His mouth trailed along her neck, lingering where her pulse fluttered beneath his lips, drawing a soft gasp from her.

"Ave…" he groaned, voice breaking, "if you keep makin' those sounds—"

She threaded her fingers into his hair, pulling him closer. "Don't stop."

He exhaled like he couldn't breathe without her.

Logan lowered her onto the couch, hovering above her as if giving her one last chance to run. She didn't. She curled her hand around the back of his neck, tugging him down to her again.

"Tell me what you want," he whispered.

"You," she breathed. "Just you."

His forehead pressed to hers, his voice raw. "Then I'm yours."

The world outside blurred into wind and snow. Inside, everything softened—his touch, his breath, the way he whispered her name like it was something sacred. The fire crackled beside them, casting shifting patterns of gold across their bodies as they moved together with slow, deliberate closeness.

Avery felt herself unravel in waves—gentle, consuming, safe.

And Logan held her through every one.

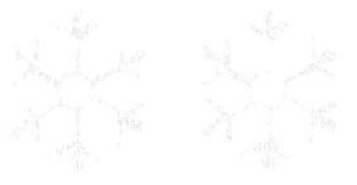

Later, they lay tangled on the couch, the fire burning low. Logan drew lazy circles along her arm with his thumb, his breath warm against her hair.

"You know," he said quietly, "I used to think I wasn't built for this."

"For what?" she asked softly.

"Letting someone close." His voice dipped. "Every time I tried, it ended with me wonderin' what part of me wasn't enough."

Her heart clenched. Not at his words—but at the pain beneath them.

"Logan…"

"But with you," he whispered, voice unsteady, "it doesn't feel like pretending. And that scares the hell outta me."

She brushed her fingers against his cheek. "You're not the only one scared."

He exhaled, a soft, shaky surrender. "Then maybe we can be scared together."

Avery smiled faintly, pressing her forehead to his. "That's the bravest thing I've heard all week."

Outside, the wind roared through the pines, though the cabin felt warm, and alive with something beyond mere heat.

Hope.

The thought terrified her—because choosing him meant letting herself hope again.

She wasn't falling in love by accident.

She was choosing it.

Chapter 21

Holiday Chaos, Private Moments

The first clear morning in nearly a week dawned bright and cold, sunlight spilling across the snow like spilled sugar. Avery woke to the sound of laughter—dozens of voices, car doors slamming, the scrape of boots on the porch.

She blinked, momentarily disoriented. Logan's arm was still around her, his body solid and warm against her back. The fire had burned to embers, and the cabin smelled faintly of coffee and cedar.

He groaned softly when she shifted. "Don't move," he murmured, voice low and gravelly from sleep.

"Logan," she whispered, "there are people outside."

He opened one eye, expression slow to register. Then, as the realization hit, he cursed softly and sat up. "Hell. My family's early."

Avery froze. "Your family?"

"Yeah. My sister said they'd swing by before Christmas to check on the ranch." Logan scrubbed a hand through his hair, making it even more of a disaster. "I, uh… might've forgotten to mention we'd be snowed in."

"Or sharing a bed," Avery muttered, tugging the blanket up to her chin like it could erase the night they'd just had.

Logan's grin appeared instantly—slow, wicked, devastating.
 "Kinda what married people do, sweetheart."

"Logan!" She grabbed a pillow and hurled it at him.

He caught it without even blinking. "What? I'm just sayin', my family's not gonna think anything's weird. Honestly, we'd look suspicious if we *weren't* a little… rumpled."

Avery gaped at him. "Suspicious? Logan, I look like I lost a fight with your shirt."

He glanced at her—hair a mess, cheeks flushed, swimming in his flannel.
 His smirk turned downright sinful.
 "So… adorable?"

"Absolutely not."

"Sexy as hell?"

"Logan."

"Fine, fine." He lifted his hands in surrender. "Cute and devastatingly distracting."

She threw the second pillow at his head. He ducked, laughing.

"This isn't funny!" she snapped, mostly because he wouldn't stop smiling like he'd won something.

"Relax, Doc," he drawled. "My family already thinks we're happily married. Us lookin' like we actually enjoy each other? That just sells it."

She pointed at him accusingly. "I am not walking out of this room looking like I just—"
 She gestured vaguely at him.
 "—fell out of your arms."

His grin sharpened. "Fell out, huh? Not… crawled into?"

She nearly choked. "LOGAN HUNTER."

"What?" he asked innocently. "You started it."

"I absolutely did NOT!"

"You said arms."

"That does not count!"

He shrugged. "Sounds like it counts."

She groaned dramatically and flopped back against the bed. "Why are you like this?"

He leaned over her, bracing one arm on the mattress. "Genetics. Cowboy blood. Natural charm. Want me to keep goin'?"

"No," she said flatly.

"Yes," he teased, brushing a curl from her face.

Her blush deepened. "Logan, seriously. Your family already thinks this marriage is real. Can you please try—just for two minutes—not to make this harder?"

His expression shifted—softening, deepening, turning her stomach into knots.
 "Sweetheart… me bein' in the same room as you is what makes it harder."

Her breath *stopped.*
 Entirely.

He winked. "See? You started that one too."

She shoved him off the bed so fast he actually hit the floor.
"OW—hey!"

"Get dressed," she ordered, pointing to his jeans, "before I walk out of here and tell your family the marriage is fake out of sheer spite."

He scrambled up, laughing. "You wouldn't."

"Watch me."

"You're cute when you're threatening me."

"AND YOU ARE INCREDIBLY—"
She pointed at him again, flustered and furious.
"—YOU."

Logan tugged his shirt over his head, still smirking. "That's the best compliment I've ever gotten."

"No, it's not."

"It is now."

"Out. GO."

"Yes, ma'am," he said, shooting her one last wicked grin. "Don't forget—you're the one wearin' my shirt."

He shut the door behind him.

Avery threw a pillow at it anyway.

By the time they stepped outside, the yard was full of life. Trucks lined the driveway, kids were throwing snowballs, and a golden retriever bounded toward Logan with a wagging tail. His younger sister, Maddie, was unloading boxes from a truck, her breath clouding in the air.

"About time you two showed up!" she called, grinning. "Thought the newlyweds froze to death up here."

Avery choked. "Newly—what?"

Logan shot her a warning glance, slipping an arm casually around her waist. "Hey, Mads. Good to see you too."

Maddie raised a brow, delighted by the sight of them. "Wow. Guess the rumors were true. You actually settled down."

"Something like that," Logan said smoothly. His hand squeezed Avery's waist: a silent go with it.

Avery forced a smile. "He's been very…persuasive."

Maddie laughed. "I bet he has."

Logan cleared his throat. "Why don't you all come inside? I'll get the fire going."

As family members filed toward the cabin, Avery leaned close and murmured, "You could've warned me I was meeting the entire Hunter family."

He snorted. "They don't really do warning shots."

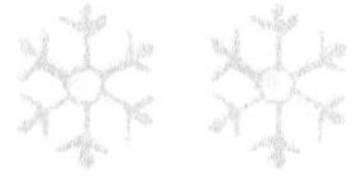

Logan's POV

Logan barely made it two steps inside before the noise hit him—his mother fussing with the garland, his cousins arguing over who dumped flour on who, the dog skidding across the wood floor like a drunken deer. The whole damn house vibrated with Hunter-family chaos.

He should've been used to it. He grew up in this storm.

But today felt different.

Because Avery was in the middle of it.

His Avery.

Not his wife. Not really. But she moved through the room like she belonged here—like she'd always belonged here—smiling shyly as his mother pinned a sprig of pine to her sweater, laughing softly as Maddie teased her about "wrangling a cowboy."

And something in Logan's chest… shifted. Tensed. Softened. All at once.

He leaned against the doorframe, arms crossed, watching her with a focus he didn't bother to hide. The fire caught her curls, making them glow like warm copper. Her cheeks were flushed from the cold. She kept brushing the sleeve of his flannel like she was remembering last night and trying not to show it.

Damn, she had no idea what she did to him.

Maddie bumped his shoulder. "You're staring. It's embarrassing."

Logan grunted. "Mind your business."

Maddie smirked. "So you are in love."

He glared at her. "Drop it."

But she didn't wipe that knowing smile off her face—and it made his pulse spike. Because he was playing a part. Supposed to be pretending.

Only it didn't feel like pretending anymore.

He rubbed a hand over his jaw and tried to shake it off. He didn't get attached. He didn't catch feelings. He didn't let someone slip under his skin like this.

Yet here he was—heart kicking like a damn spooked horse every time she laughed.

When Karen Whitman pulled Avery aside to chat, Logan's eyes narrowed instantly. He didn't trust that woman as far as he could throw her. And when Karen leaned in too close, voice dropping into that fake-sweet gossip tone Avery hated—

Logan was across the room before he realized he'd moved.

His hand slid to Avery's waist automatically, his thumb brushing the soft knit of her sweater. She stiffened for a second… then relaxed into him like it was the most natural thing in the world.

That tiny lean?

It wrecked him.

"You need anything, sweetheart?" he murmured, letting the endearment curl warm and protective around them both.

Avery looked up at him, eyes softening. "I'm fine."

But Logan wasn't. Not even close.

She fit against him too perfectly. Too easily. Like she was made to be there.

Careful, he told himself. Keep your head straight.

Because he was dangerously close to forgetting why this started.

He watched her all afternoon—teaching the kids how to roll dough, laughing with Maddie, spinning with him near the fire during that song that hit a little too close to home. His hand on her waist, her breath catching when he dipped her—

He wanted more. A hell of a lot more.

And later, when her fingers brushed his hand as she reached for cocoa, when her eyes met his like she already knew what he was thinking—

Logan realized exactly how screwed he was.

He wasn't pretending for her family.

He was pretending for himself.

Trying to believe he could pull away when this was over.

Trying—and failing—not to fall for the woman who made his whole damn world feel like it'd been waiting for her.

When he finally whispered, "Meet me outside," it wasn't part of the act.

He just needed her.
 He needed ten minutes alone. Ten breaths. Ten seconds to touch her without pretending, even if neither of them said the truth out loud.

And when she followed him into the cold, wrapped in his jacket like it belonged on her shoulders—

Logan knew.
 Dangerously.
 Irrevocably.

He wasn't falling.
He'd already fallen.

Avery stepped toward him, breath fogging in the chill, her eyes wide and unsure and wanting in a way that punched the air from his lungs. "Logan… are you okay?"

"No," he murmured. His voice came out rough. Honest. Too honest. "Not even close."

She froze, snow settling in her hair like tiny crystals. "What does that mean?"

He didn't answer. Couldn't.
 Instead, he reached up, fingers brushing a strand of hair from her cheek. She leaned into the touch almost without realizing it, her breath catching—soft, shaky, devastating.

"Avery," he whispered, as if her name alone steadied him. "I can't pretend around you anymore."

Her eyes flicked to his mouth before she could stop herself.

That was all it took.

He cupped her jaw gently—so gently it hurt—and she exhaled like she'd been holding her breath for days. The space between them dissolved, slow at first, then pulled tight like gravity snapping into place.

"Logan…" She whispered it like a warning. Or a surrender.
 He couldn't tell the difference.

"Tell me to stop," he breathed.

She didn't. She didn't even blink.

He dipped his forehead to hers, a quiet groan leaving him when she leaned into him instead of away. And then—slowly, reverently, like he was finally touching something he'd dreamed about too long—

Logan kissed her.

It wasn't rushed.
 It wasn't hungry.
 It was *inevitable.*

A warm, burning press of lips, snow melting in her hair, her fingers bunching in his jacket because she had nothing to hold on to except him. His thumb brushed her cheekbone, coaxing her closer, deepening the kiss just enough for the world to disappear beneath the snowfall.

When he finally broke away, his breath trembled against her lips.

"This isn't pretend," he whispered.

Avery's eyes fluttered open, her voice barely a breath.
 "I know."

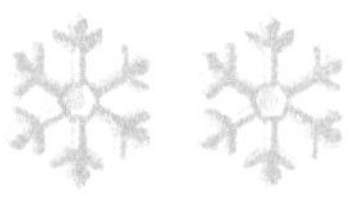

Inside, the chaos only grew louder. The cabin was overflowing within minutes. Kids dumped their bags everywhere, cousins claimed bunk beds, and by the time Avery and Logan made it upstairs, their shared room had already been taken over by Maddie's kids.

"Guess we're in separate rooms tonight," Logan murmured, his voice low enough only she could hear.

Avery's stomach dipped. Separate rooms. After everything.

"Just for tonight," he added softly, brushing her hand before stepping down the hall. "Less explaining."

Maddie unpacked homemade pies. Logan's mother, Evelyn, rearranged the garland on the mantle. Two cousins argued over cocoa.

Avery stood by the kitchen counter, slightly overwhelmed. This was the kind of family warmth she hadn't felt in years—messy, loud, alive.

Logan noticed, sliding beside her until the heat of him steadied her. "You okay?"

She nodded. "Just… not used to this."

His gaze softened. "Yeah. It's a lot. But they'll love you."

"Because I'm your pretend wife," she whispered.

"Because you're you," he corrected gently.

Her stomach fluttered.

Logan noticed—of course he did. His eyes softened, that quiet kind of warmth that made her chest ache. And when no one was looking, he slid a hand across the counter until his fingertips brushed hers.

Avery inhaled.
Slow.
Shaky.

"Logan…" she whispered, unsure whether it was a warning or a plea.

He leaned in—just an inch—just enough that the smell of cedar and winter and him filled her senses. "C'mere," he murmured, so soft she barely heard it over the chaos.

Before she could stop herself, she stepped closer.

His hand came to her waist. Hers found the collar of his flannel. And in the middle of clattering dishes, kid laughter, and the smell of homemade pie—

Logan kissed her.

Not wild.
Not rushed.
Just warm, deep, and real enough to make her forget the world existed for three whole seconds.

She melted into him—actually melted—and he smiled against her lips like he couldn't help it. His thumb brushed her cheek, her hand curled in his shirt, and they were both so lost in each other—

"EW, UNCLE LOGAN!"

Avery jolted so hard she nearly knocked over the cocoa tin.

Two kids stood in the doorway, wide-eyed, scandalized, and absolutely delighted.

"Grandma!" one yelled. "They're kissing in the kitchen!"

A chorus of gasps, laughs, and footsteps followed as the entire family swarmed like happy vultures.

Maddie leaned in, hands on her hips. "Well, well, well. Guess someone's enjoying married life."

Avery's face went up in flames. "W—we were just—um—he—"

Evelyn, Logan's mother, clasped her hands together with a dreamy sigh. "Oh, look at her blush! Logan, stop teasing your wife."

Avery's soul left her body. "I—he— we—"

Logan slipped an arm around her waist like he'd been waiting for this moment his entire life, smug and annoyingly unbothered.

"Sorry," he said, not sounding sorry at all. "Couldn't help myself."

"Clearly," one cousin laughed. "You two need a warning label."

The kids giggled. Maddie elbowed Logan. Evelyn winked at Avery.
And Avery?

She ducked her head, face burning, heart thundering, hiding behind Logan's shoulder like it was a shield.

Logan leaned down, voice low enough only she could hear.
"Relax, Doc," he murmured, lips brushing her ear. "They already adore you."

Avery peeked up—her cheeks still blazing—and saw it:

Smiles.
Laughter.
Affection.
No judgment.
Just a family who embraced her like she belonged.

And Logan…
Logan couldn't stop looking at her like he knew she did.

The morning blurred into an afternoon of baking and decorating. Evelyn insisted on teaching Avery how to make the family's secret cinnamon rolls, while Logan attempted—unsuccessfully—to keep children from launching flour grenades.

Someone turned on music. Maddie grabbed Logan's sleeve. "Dance with your wife, cowboy!"

Avery's eyes widened. "Oh, no, I don't—"

But Logan already had her hand, pulling her toward the fire. The music was soft, an old country love song, and suddenly they were swaying together, slow and close.

"You don't have to play along that hard," she whispered, though her hands were already on his chest.

"Who's pretending?" he murmured.

Her pulse fluttered. His breath brushed her ear as he guided her through the steps, fingers warm at the small of her back.

For a moment, the world shrank to just them.

Then Maddie whistled, and Avery flushed scarlet. Logan chuckled, spinning her gently. "You're a natural."

"You're insufferable."

But she was smiling.

By evening, the family chaos peaked. Evelyn declared everyone was staying for dinner, and the long table filled with laughter, spilled gravy, and stories of Logan's childhood mischief.

Avery laughed more that night than she had in months.

But beneath the joy, the tension simmered—stolen glances, the brush of hands, the memory of last night's closeness warm beneath her skin.

When dinner ended and board games began, Logan brushed past her, fingers grazing her lower back.

"Meet me outside," he whispered.

Her breath caught. "Logan—your family—"

"They'll survive ten minutes without me."

Avery hesitated only a moment before slipping out the side door.

Outside, the world was quiet again. Snow glowed under the moonlight, untouched and perfect. Cold nipped her cheeks, but Logan's jacket was around her shoulders before she could shiver.

"You're impossible," she whispered, pulling it tight.

"Maybe," he said, stepping close, "but you like it."

She looked up at him. "Your family's going to notice we're gone."

"Let 'em." His voice dropped. "They think we're married anyway."

Her heart stumbled. "You're enjoying this way too much."

His smile was soft, dangerous. "You have no idea."

The air grew heavy. She could hear muffled laughter from inside, but it felt worlds away. Logan lifted a hand to her cheek, his touch warm against the winter air.

"You fit here," he said quietly. "More than you think."

"Logan…"

He swallowed. "I know we started this pretend. But when I see you with them… it feels real. Like I've had this all along and didn't know it."

Her breath shook. "You shouldn't say things like that."

"Why not?"

"Because I'll start believing you."

He stepped closer, their breath mingling. "Maybe you should."

A shiver rolled through her—not from the cold, but from the way he was looking at her. That heavy, unguarded want he never bothered to hide around her anymore.

"Logan," she whispered, breath fogging between them, "someone could come out here."

"Then we'll be quick," he murmured, "or quiet."

Before she could respond, his hand slid to the back of her neck, guiding her toward him. The kiss wasn't gentle—it was deep, warm, hungry enough to thaw the winter air. Avery's fingers curled into his jacket, pulling him closer.

Logan groaned softly into her mouth, the sound low and undone.

"Sweetheart," he breathed, lips brushing hers, "you have no idea what you do to me."

His hand traced her waist, pulling her flush against him. Heat shot through her, her breath catching on a soft, involuntary sound.

He tensed. "Don't do that."

Her eyes widened. "Why?"

He lowered his forehead to hers, breathing hard. "Because I'll forget my family's ten feet away. And I'll take you right inside the barn and lock the damn door."

Her knees nearly gave.

He kissed her again—slow this time, lingering, tender. Snowflakes clung to his lashes as he pulled back enough to look at her.

"You feel like home," he whispered.

Her chest ached. "Logan…"

He kissed beneath her ear, soft and warm. "Tell me this doesn't feel real."

She couldn't. Not even if she wanted to.

Her fingers gripped his shirt. "It feels too real."

"Good," he whispered. "Then I'm not the only one losin' my mind."

A door creaked from inside. They froze.

Logan steadied her, brushing her cheek with one last touch. "Later," he murmured. "When it's just us."

And God help her—she wanted that more than anything.

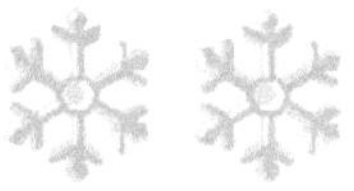

Inside, chaos resumed—hot cocoa refills, Christmas movies, kids passed out in a pile of blankets. But every time Avery met Logan's gaze across the room, she felt it again: that magnetic pull, impossible to ignore.

Later, when she slipped into the guest room, she found Logan already there, sitting on the edge of the bed, running a hand through his hair.

"Long night," he said with a tired grin.

"You think?" she teased lightly.

He looked up, expression softening. "You were incredible with them tonight. My mom hasn't smiled that much in years."

Emotion tightened her throat. "They're good people, Logan. You can tell they love you."

"Yeah," he said quietly. "But they like you too. Maybe more."

Avery laughed gently. "You're ridiculous."

"Maybe." He nodded toward her. "But I mean it."

Silence settled between them, warm but charged. Avery wrapped the blanket tighter around her shoulders, unsure what to do with her hands… or her heart.

"You should get some sleep," she murmured.

He stood, stepping close enough that she could feel his breath. "If I do, I'll dream about you anyway."

Her pulse stumbled. "Logan—"

He pressed a soft kiss to her temple. "Goodnight, Doc."

And then he slipped out the door.

Avery stood frozen, staring at the space he left behind—because she knew, without a doubt:

Nothing about this was pretend anymore.

Not one single thing.

Chapter 22

Forbidden Longings

The next morning dawned soft and bright, sunlight spilling across the snow and filtering through the cabin's frosted windows. The storm had finally passed, but inside, the air still buzzed with quiet electricity — the kind holiday chatter could never drown out.

Avery woke to the scent of coffee and cinnamon, the distant hum of voices drifting through the hall. Her pulse stuttered before her mind caught up.

Right.

Logan's family was still here.

The other side of the bed was empty but still faintly warm — the kind of reminder she absolutely did not need.

Downstairs, laughter echoed through the kitchen. When she walked in, Logan stood at the stove, sleeves rolled up, flipping pancakes like he'd been designed in a "hot cowboy husband" factory. Sunlight caught in the golden streaks of his hair, and the sight hit her hard in the chest.

He glanced over, caught her staring, and that slow, wicked grin curved his lips.

"Mornin', Doc. Sleep all right?"

"Barely," she muttered, reaching for a mug to keep her hands busy.

"Can't imagine why," he said, flipping a pancake. "You didn't seem to have any trouble drifting off last night."

She shot him a look. "You mean before or after you whispered goodnight like it was a threat?"

His smirk deepened. "Depends. Did it keep you awake?"

Her fingers tightened around her mug. "You're annoying."

"And yet…" He leaned in, breath brushing her ear. "…you keep looking at me like you forgot how to breathe."

Her pulse jumped violently.

Before she could assemble a comeback, the kitchen door swung open and Maddie breezed in, cheeks pink from the cold.

"Okay, who wants to go sledding? Dad says the hill behind the barn is perfect!"

Avery stepped back so fast she nearly spilled her coffee. Logan bit back a laugh.

"I'm out," he said. "Someone's gotta clean up after you hooligans."

Maddie rolled her eyes. "Fine, Grandpa. Avery, you coming?"

"I—uh—maybe later," Avery said, trying to sound normal.

When Maddie disappeared, Avery let out a breath. Logan chuckled low under his breath.

"You really are bad at hiding it."

"Hiding what?" she snapped a little too quickly.

He tilted his head, eyes dark and knowing. "The fact that you want me even when you shouldn't."

Her heart slammed. "You're imagining things."

"Am I?"

He stepped in closer, the space shrinking between them.

"Because every time I walk into a room, you stop breathing. Every time I touch you, you freeze like you're afraid everyone's going to see what's all over your face."

Her cheeks burned. "Logan—your family's here."

He smiled faintly — like that was half the problem, half the thrill.

"Exactly."

The day unfolded in bursts of sound and laughter. Logan's family filled every corner of the cabin — shrieking kids, cookies cooling on racks, Christmas music competing with conversation.

Avery and Logan orbited each other like magnets trying — and failing — not to collide.

At lunch, she caught him watching her from across the room, gaze slow and deliberate. It made her throat go dry.

When she reached for a tray of rolls, he appeared behind her, too close, too warm.

"You missed one," he murmured, brushing a piece of dough from her wrist.

She turned too fast — her chest brushing his, her breath catching.

The tray wobbled in her hands.

He steadied it with one hand, eyes locked on hers.

"Careful, sweetheart."

Avery swallowed. "I think you're the one making a mess."

"Maybe," he whispered, leaning in just enough. "But I've got no regrets about it."

His hand was still on hers — warm, steady, entirely too intentional.

Avery should've stepped away.

She didn't.

Logan's thumb brushed the inside of her wrist, slow and claiming, sending a shiver all the way up her arm. His body pinned her gently against the counter, not quite touching — but close enough that her breath stalled.

"Logan…" she whispered.

"Yeah?" he murmured, eyes dropping to her mouth.

She shouldn't.

He shouldn't.

His whole family was ten feet away.

And yet—

His fingers slid lightly up her forearm, leaving goosebumps in their wake. "You keep looking at me like that," he said quietly, "and I'm gonna forget we're supposed to be on our best behavior."

Her breath trembled. "We're not on any behavior."

"That's the problem."

Just as his lips brushed her cheek, the kitchen door swung open.

Evelyn bustled in, humming carols, oblivious to the fire crackling between them.

Avery jerked back so fast she nearly dropped the tray. Logan bit down a laugh, reaching for a dish towel like nothing happened.

"Relax, sweetheart," he murmured under his breath. "We're just making lunch."

"You're going to get us caught, again" she hissed.

He winked. "Worth it."

That afternoon, Logan and his brother went out to chop wood while the rest of the family prepped dinner. Avery joined Maddie in decorating cookies, though her focus kept drifting toward the window — to where Logan worked shirtless beneath the pale winter sun.

Snow on his shoulders.

Sweat at his temple.

Muscles flexing with every swing of the axe.

Maddie caught her staring and snorted. "Careful. That's how you get roped into helping him stack it."

Avery flushed. "I was just… checking to make sure he doesn't hurt himself."

"Sure you were," Maddie teased. "You look at him like he's a walking Christmas wish."

Avery's face went hot.

"He's your brother."

"Exactly," Maddie said, smirking. "I know trouble when I see it."

By sunset, the house was buzzing again. Music. Kids. Food. Chaos.

Logan sat beside Avery on the couch, his arm draped along the backrest. Every time he shifted, his fingertips brushed the back of her neck.

It was maddening.

"You're doing that on purpose," she whispered.

"Doing what?" he asked, eyes still on the TV.

"Touching me."

"Maybe," he said. "But I think you like it."

She turned her head toward him. His gaze met hers — slow, loaded, electric.

Her pulse hiccuped.

His fingers brushed the top of her spine again — featherlight but intentional. Avery's breath caught.

Logan leaned in, voice low enough that only she could hear.

"You feel that too, right?"

"Logan…" she warned.

"What? The way you keep leaning into me?"

His lips ghosted the shell of her ear. "Or the way you want to."

Her whole body warmed. "Your family—"

"Isn't looking," he murmured, brushing a knuckle down her jaw.

Avery swallowed, unable to look away from his eyes.

He looked hungry.

Focused.

Like she was the only thing in the room.

His hand cupped her cheek, thumb brushing her bottom lip.

"Tell me not to," he whispered.

She didn't.

He leaned in—

And a pillow flew across the room, smacking Logan in the side of the head.

Avery nearly shot off the couch. Logan caught the pillow midair, laughing with the kids like he hadn't just been moments from kissing her senseless.

His hand slid off her neck — reluctantly.

Her heart thudded against her ribs.

Later, after the family drifted to bed, the cabin finally quieted.

Avery lingered by the fire, staring into the flames as they shifted gold and ember.

Logan joined her, voice a low murmur. "You've been quiet tonight."

"Just thinking."

"About?"

"You."

He stilled. "Yeah?"

She nodded. "About how this is supposed to be pretend… but it doesn't feel like it anymore. And it scares me."

He stepped close enough that their hands brushed. "You think it doesn't scare me?"

"I think you like it too much to be scared."

His smile was soft, sad, loaded. "You'd be surprised, Doc. I've wanted things before — but not like this."

The fire cracked.

"Logan," she whispered, "your family is right upstairs."

He looked at her, eyes dark and tender. "Then we'll have to be quiet."

He leaned in — just enough to brush his lips along her jaw, soft and devastating — and Avery's breath left her in one broken sound.

They pulled apart only when footsteps creaked overhead.

Avery jumped.

Logan smiled faintly, thumb brushing the corner of her mouth.

"Another close call."

"You're going to get us caught," she breathed.

He shook his head slowly. "Tell me you don't want to be caught."

She glared weakly. "You're infuriating."

"And you're beautiful when you're mad."

"Go to bed, Logan."

He leaned in, voice a warm whisper. "You first, Doc. Or I'll think you like having me this close."

A shiver rolled through her.

"Goodnight, Logan."

He chuckled softly, stepping away — but his hand grazed her wrist, a fleeting, dangerous touch that lingered long after he disappeared down the hall.

That night, Avery lay awake listening to the wind rattle the windows and her heartbeat thundering against the quiet.

Every inch of her still felt him.

His hands.

His breath.

His almost-kisses.

It wasn't just desire anymore.

It was something heavier.

Hotter.

More terrifying.

Down the hall, she could hear faint footsteps —
Logan's, pacing restlessly in his own room.

They were both awake.

Both wanting.

Both afraid.

And neither of them, Avery knew, was pretending
anymore.

Just as Avery finally drifted toward sleep,
headlights flashed against the frost on her window
— bright enough to make her sit upright.

At nearly 1 a.m.?

Her pulse spiked.

Then came voices. Familiar ones.

Her mother's.

"Oh my goodness, look at all this snow! Do you think they're asleep? Nate, carry the bags—don't drag them!"

Avery's blood ran cold.

"Oh no…" she breathed.

Doors slammed. Footsteps crunched toward the cabin.

Her father's voice followed, muffled but unmistakable.

"I told you not to surprise them. This is rude, Patrice—"

"It's family!" her mother snapped. "We can arrive whenever we want! We're staying the rest of the week!"

Avery slapped a hand over her mouth.

"Oh. My. God."

The front door creaked open — and her mother's bright voice pierced the quiet:

"Avery! Logan! We're home!"

Across the hall, another door opened.

Logan stepped out, shirtless, hair messy, frozen in the doorway.

His eyes met hers.

His voice dropped to a horrified whisper.

"Sweetheart… your family just walked in."

Avery groaned.

"Kill me now."

Chapter 23

Christmas Eve Heat

Earlier That Evening…

Christmas Eve on the ranch felt like the kind of chaos that only happened in stories—a joyful storm of laughter, snow boots, cocoa mugs, and too many people talking at once.

Avery's family blended into Logan's as if they'd been doing holidays together for decades. Logan's sisters chatted with Avery's mother. The cousins invented a sledding competition. Kids raced through the cabin with icing in their hair. Someone put on old Christmas records that popped and crackled.

It should've been overwhelming.
 It was.
 But Avery couldn't stop smiling.

Just as Logan walked in with more firewood, the front door banged open.

A hush rippled through the room.

Logan froze mid-step—then his face broke into a grin so bright it stunned Avery.

"Papaw."

A tall, weather-worn man stepped through the doorway, red-cheeked from the cold, shaking snow off his hat. His eyes glittered with mischief, warmth, and the kind of quiet strength that made everything around him feel steadier.

Papaw.

Avery felt the weight of the moment. Logan hadn't spoken of him often, but when he had… it was with reverence.

Papaw grabbed Logan in a one-armed hug, patting his back so hard Avery swore she heard bones crack.
 "Boy, these roads are a death trap. Almost got myself stuck behind a drift bigger'n your mama."

Evelyn gasped. "Dad!"

Papaw winked.

Then his gaze fell on Avery.

He didn't look her over.
 He *saw* her.

"And you must be Miss Avery," he said with a slow, knowing smile. "Been hearin' a whole lot about you."

Avery flushed. "All good things, I hope."

"Oh, honey." Papaw chuckled, patting her hand. "Logan don't talk much. If he mentioned you at all? Means he's sweet on you."

Logan choked on air.
"Papaw—seriously? We talked about this."

"Nope," Papaw replied. "I talk when I want."

Avery laughed nervously, covering her burning cheeks.

The kids immediately swarmed Papaw like moths to a flame.
 "Tell us a story!"
 "Tell us when Uncle Logan got bucked off a horse!"
 "Did he cry?"
 "Did he scream?"

Papaw settled into the rocking chair, dramatically adjusting his hat.
 "Alright now," he said with a stern face that fooled no one. "I'll tell you 'bout the time yer Uncle Logan

tried to ride a bull that had more attitude than his mama before coffee—"

"Papaw!" Logan's sisters gasped. "Don't listen to him, kids!"

Papaw ignored them and launched into the story.

Logan groaned into his hands.
 Avery giggled.
And the kids howled with laughter through the whole tale, especially when Papaw reenacted Logan flying through the air.

Later, Avery found herself chatting with one of Logan's cousins near the fireplace.
 He was friendly, charming, and harmless.

Logan walked by, glanced once, and—

Stopped.

He didn't say anything.
 Didn't glare.
 Didn't growl.

But the muscle in his jaw ticked.
 His hand closed around the back of a chair a little too tightly.
 And his eyes tracked Avery the entire time, like his body refused to look away.

When the cousin laughed at something Avery said, Logan suddenly appeared at her side.

"Hey, Doc," he said, voice casual-but-not. "Need help with… anything?"

Avery blinked. "No? We were just—"

"We'll talk later," the cousin said, patting Logan on the shoulder as he wandered off.

Logan waited until he was out of earshot.
 "Didn't like how he looked at you," he muttered, barely audible.

"Logan," she whispered, "he was being friendly."

"Uh-huh," he said, clearly not convinced.

Her heart did a weird, warm somersault.

From the sofa, Avery observed Logan and Papaw's hushed discussion near the window.
 She couldn't hear their words, but the sight alone hit her harder than expected.

Papaw's hand rested on Logan's shoulder.
Logan's head dipped, almost shy.
His expression softened into something she'd never seen—raw, unguarded, boyish.

Avery realized then:

Logan wasn't just strong.
He wasn't just charming.
He wasn't just desire and heat and trouble.

He was vulnerability.
History.
Love.
A man shaped by the people who surrounded him.

A man who looked at her like she was already part
of that world.

Her chest tightened.

She wasn't ready for that truth…
But it was here.

When the crowd thinned, Papaw nudged Logan
outside onto the porch.

"Boy," he said in a low voice, snow crunching
beneath their boots, "you're lookin' at that girl like
she hung the moon."

Logan swallowed. "Papaw, don't start."

"I've already started. Now hush."
Papaw leaned against the railing. "I ain't seen you
this happy since you were ten and found that stray
puppy."

Logan huffed. "This is different."

"Yeah," Papaw said. "It's real. That's what scares you."

Logan's chest tightened. "She deserves better than… all this." He gestured vaguely at himself, the ranch, the chaos.

Papaw snorted. "You listen here. That woman ain't lookin' at the ranch."
 He tapped Logan's chest.
 "She's lookin' at *you.*"

Logan's breath hitched, caught between fear and hope.

Papaw smirked. "Now go inside before you freeze yer butt off. And don't be an idiot. If you love her, let her see it."

Logan almost choked. "I didn't say I love—"

Papaw was already inside.

By the time the families drifted upstairs, full and happy, Avery curled up on the couch in Logan's flannel. Logan lingered by the staircase, watching her with a look that made her entire body heat.

Neither of them said anything.

They didn't have to.

Something was changing.

Something inevitable.

Something neither could pretend away.

The world outside was wrapped in silence.

Snow drifted past the cabin windows like flakes of glass, glinting beneath the soft glow of the Christmas lights on the porch. Inside, the fire burned low and steady, throwing warm orange light across the room.

It was late — long past midnight.

Most of the house was asleep, the kind of exhausted, joyful sleep that came after too many games, too much sugar, and laughter bright enough to warm the winter.

Maddie had been one of the last to finally go upstairs.

Before she disappeared down the hall, she paused at the bottom of the steps and looked over her shoulder.

Her eyes lingered on Avery curled on the couch in Logan's flannel…and the way Logan had tried — and failed — not to watch Avery all night.

Maddie's brow pinched, thoughtful.

Earlier she'd noticed Avery flinching when Logan's mother called her "Mrs. Hunter."

And she'd watched Logan stiffen when Avery's brother teased him about "marrying a doctor on impulse."

She didn't say anything.

But she saw everything.

With one last sharp glance between the two of them, Maddie headed upstairs..

Everyone except Avery.

She curled on the couch in one of Logan's old flannels, knees drawn to her chest, staring at the flickering fire. The quiet hum of the storm outside matched the restlessness twisting in her chest.

No matter how she tried, she couldn't quiet her thoughts — or the way her skin still remembered his hands.

It had been days since their last stolen moment. But every brush of his fingers, every look that lingered too long, clung to her like heat beneath the cold.

The floor creaked.

Avery turned, pulse leaping — and there he was.

Logan.

Barefoot, half-asleep, a loose T-shirt clinging to his chest.

His hair tousled, his voice rough and softened with sleep.

"Can't sleep either?"

"Guess not," she said quietly.

He crossed the room and sank onto the couch beside her — close enough that she could feel the warmth radiating off his body.

"Too much sugar," he teased, "or too much thinking?"

"Both."

A slow smile tugged at his lips. "Storm's rollin' in again. Looks like we're stuck another day."

Avery swallowed. "You sound disappointed."

"Not even a little."

Silence stretched — soft, electric.

The fire popped.

"Everyone's asleep," he murmured, voice lower now. "Feels weird. Like the world's… holding its breath."

"Maybe it is," she whispered.

Upstairs, a door creaked. Maddie stepped halfway down the staircase, unseen, looking between them.

Avery on the couch, flushed and restless.

Logan drifted toward her like he couldn't stay away.

Maddie's arms folded slowly.

Something wasn't adding up.

They acted like a couple falling hard…but earlier, every time someone mentioned wedding details or their first date, they both had looked lost.

Her eyes narrowed, sharpened.

They're hiding something.

She waited one more beat — watching Logan sit beside Avery, the air between them practically glowing — then slipped quietly back upstairs.

Their eyes met — and held.

Too long.

Too deep.

Too honest.

He shifted, knee brushing hers, small but intentional.

"You've been avoiding me," he said.

"I have not."

"Liar." His smile was quiet, knowing. "You barely look at me when anyone's around."

"That's because your mother already looks at me like I'm about to ruin Christmas."

He laughed under his breath. "She likes you."

"Logan—"

"I mean it." He turned toward her fully. "She thinks you're good for me."

Avery blinked. "Good for you? We're supposed to be pretending."

Something flickered in his expression — a vulnerability he rarely let anyone see.

"Yeah," he said softly. "We were."

The words dropped heavy between them.

Warm.

Dangerous.

True.

Logan reached out, tracing one fingertip down her arm.

Goosebumps erupted instantly.

"Tell me to stop," he whispered.

She didn't.

She couldn't.

He tilted her chin with his knuckles, slow and reverent, and the tiny breath she took disappeared entirely.

Then he kissed her.

Soft at first, like he was memorizing the shape of her mouth.

Then deeper when she leaned in, her fingers sliding instinctively into his hair.

Logan's breath caught against her lips.

"I've wanted this," he whispered, voice breaking just slightly, "since the first time you told me not to."

Her voice trembled. "You don't even know what this is."

His forehead rested against hers.

"Then let's find out."

The kiss deepened, unraveling slowly, like both of them had been starving and didn't know how to pace themselves anymore.

Logan guided her gently backward until her back met the cushions, but he didn't climb over her — not yet. Instead, he kissed a path down her jaw, her throat, each touch warm enough to steal her breath.

"Avery…" he murmured against her skin. "Tell me you want this."

She tugged him closer, voice shaking. "I do."

His exhale hit her like heat.

He settled above her, bracing himself with one arm, his other hand sliding along her waist — slow, careful, reverent — as if he were learning her by touch alone. She arched into him on instinct, and he dropped his head with a quiet groan.

"Sweetheart…" His voice was wrecked.

"You're gonna undo me."

She kissed him again — deeper, hungrier — her fingers curling in the fabric of his shirt. Logan's hand traced her ribs, her hips, the curve of her thigh through the soft flannel she wore. Each touch melted something inside her she didn't know she'd been holding tight.

He paused just long enough to search her eyes.

"You okay?"

"More than okay," she whispered.

Logan's smile was soft, breathless, almost disbelieving.

"Good," he whispered, his lips brushing her ear. "Cause I'm not holdin' back anymore."

The rest unfolded in firelight and slow breaths — warm skin, tangled limbs, whispered confessions that slipped out between kisses. Logan touched her like he was memorizing everything, and Avery pulled him closer like she'd been waiting years for this moment.

It was slow.

Intense.

A giving in and a coming-undone all at once.

And when they finally stilled, tangled beneath the blanket he'd pulled over them, the fire glowing faintly across their skin, neither rushed to move.

It felt too real to break.

Afterward, the world seemed impossibly still.

Avery lay against him, her cheek resting over his heartbeat — steady, warm, safe in a way she wasn't ready to examine. Logan stroked his fingers through her hair slowly, like he didn't want to stop touching her.

For a long time, neither spoke.

Then his voice broke the quiet, soft and unsure.

"You okay?"

She smiled faintly. "You're asking me that now?"

He laughed quietly, brushing a strand of hair from her face. "You looked like you might've forgotten how to breathe for a minute."

"You did that to me," she whispered.

He smiled — but there was something deeper behind it. Something vulnerable.

"Avery…"

He hesitated.

Then: "I don't think I can go back to pretending anymore."

Her heart squeezed. "Logan—"

"I'm serious." His voice was low, rough. "This was supposed to be simple. But it's not. You make me want things I haven't let myself want in a long time."

She swallowed hard. "You don't have to say that just because—"

"I'm not."

He cupped her cheek gently.

"I'm saying it because it's true."

The words settled in her chest — heavy, terrifying, hopeful.

"Don't make promises you can't keep," she whispered.

"I'm not promising anything."

His thumb brushed her lips.

"I'm just telling you what I feel."

Her eyes stung. "And what happens when this ends? When we go back to our lives and you realize this was just—"

"Don't do that," he murmured, cutting her off softly.

"Don't shrink it down so it hurts less to lose."

A tear slid down her cheek before she could stop it.

"People leave, Logan," she whispered. "They always leave."

He kissed the tear before it fell.

"Then let me stay."

A broken sound escaped her. "You can't promise that."

"I can try."

He rested his forehead against hers, breathing her in.

His fingers trailed along her arm, light and slow.

"Come here," he whispered.

She curled into him, their legs tangled beneath the blanket.

He held her like she was something fragile and precious, his touch soft and warm.

"Avery," he murmured, almost to himself, "you terrify me."

Her breath trembled. "You terrify me too."

"Good," he whispered. "At least we're scared together."

Outside, snow fell heavier — blanketing the world in white.

Inside, it was nothing but warmth and breath and two heartbeats pressed close enough to feel like one.

Avery drifted off with her hand tangled in his.

Morning came quietly.

A pale glow seeped through the windows, turning the room silver. Avery woke alone, the blanket pulled around her shoulders.

But the pillow beside her was still warm.

A folded piece of paper rested where his head had been.

Her heart stuttered as she opened it.

Logan's handwriting — messy, rushed, unmistakably his.

Didn't want to wake you.

Went to help Dad clear the driveway.

Don't overthink last night.

I meant every word.

— L

Avery pressed the note to her chest, eyes stinging as everything inside her twisted.

Somewhere between pretending and falling — she had done the one thing she swore she wouldn't.

She let him in.

Chapter 24

Morning After Fire

The first thing Avery noticed was the warmth.

Not the steady glow of the fire or the weight of blankets.
 The warmth of him.

Logan's chest rose and fell beneath her palm, slow and sure, his heartbeat a quiet knock against her fingertips. Morning light slipped pale and blue around the edges of the curtains, turning the frost on the window into a sheet of glass.

She blinked, the memories hitting in soft, devastating fragments.

His hands.
His breath.
His voice, low and rough, promising he meant every word.
The way he'd held her like she was something he couldn't—wouldn't—let go.

Avery swallowed, afraid to move, afraid to break the moment. Logan lay on his back beside her, one arm tucked under his head, the other still resting across her waist as if his body refused to forget she was there—even in sleep.

Except he wasn't asleep.

His eyes were already on her, soft and heavy-lidded in the early light. When she met his gaze, his lips curved into the smallest, sweetest smile.

"Merry Christmas," he murmured, voice rough with sleep.

Her chest squeezed. "Merry Christmas."

They stayed like that for a long, suspended heartbeat. No pretending. No performance. Just them and the quiet.

Avery's fingers curled against his chest, her thumb brushing absently along his collarbone. Logan caught her hand gently, brought it to his mouth, and pressed a slow kiss to the inside of her wrist.

Heat shivered through her.

"Last night wasn't part of the deal," she whispered.

"No," he said, eyes darkening. "It wasn't."

He held her gaze, thumb stroking her pulse point.

"But?" she asked softly.

"But I'm not sorry," he said simply. "About any of it."

Her throat tightened. "You can't just say things like that."

"Why not?"

"Because," she whispered, "it makes it impossible to pretend."

He exhaled, the sound quiet and raw. "Good. I'm tired of pretending."
 He shifted closer, their foreheads nearly touching. "Don't overthink it, Avery. I meant every word."

As if she weren't built from overthinking.

As though last night hadn't already etched itself into her bones.

A thundering stampede of feet erupted in the hallway.

"UNCLE LOGAN! IT'S CHRISTMAS!"

A small fist pounded on the bedroom door.

Avery jolted, clutching the blanket to her chest. Logan bit back a curse and scrubbed a hand over his face.

"Don't come in!" he shouted toward the door. "We're—uh—decent, but barely."

A giggle drifted through the wood. "Aunt Avery, are you in there too?"

Avery's soul left her body. "I—yes—no—maybe!"

Logan's grin turned wicked. "Definitely yes."

"Logan," she hissed.

"Alright, alright," he called. "Give us five minutes!"

More giggles. Tiny footsteps thundered away.

Avery groaned, dropping her face into the pillow. "Kill me now."

His laughter wrapped around her like another blanket. "They already love you, Doc. No takin' it back."

She peeked up at him, cheeks burning. "This is insane."

"Maybe." He brushed a strand of hair from her face, his touch lingering. "But it feels pretty right from where I'm lying."

Her heart gave a traitorous leap.

"Get dressed," she whispered. "Before they come back and drag us downstairs."

He leaned in, stealing a quick, soft kiss that stole her breath and any chance of pretending she didn't want this.

"Yes, ma'am," he murmured.

The cabin buzzed with life when they finally made it downstairs.

The smell of cinnamon rolls and bacon filled the air. Christmas music crackled through old speakers. Kids sat cross-legged around the tree, shaking wrapped boxes and arguing over whose turn it was to pass out gifts.

Logan's mom, Evelyn, hummed softly as she flipped pancakes. Avery's mother debated oven temperature with her, insisting the rolls needed "just three more minutes." Papaw had claimed his throne in the rocking chair near the fireplace, a mug of cocoa in one hand and a plate of bacon in the other.

"'Bout time," Papaw drawled when he saw them. His eyes twinkled. "Sleep well, darlin'?"

Avery nearly choked. "I—uh—yes. Thank you."

Logan coughed into his fist, shoulders shaking with suppressed laughter.

Evelyn turned, beaming. "There you are! Merry Christmas, sweetheart." She crossed the room and pressed a kiss to Avery's cheek, then swatted Logan lightly with a dish towel. "You let her sleep in while the rest of us worked."

"She needed it," Logan said easily, his hand settling at the small of Avery's back. The touch was innocent enough for family… but warm, steady, and familiar in a way that made her pulse skip. "Doctor's orders."

Avery shot him a look. He only smiled.

Her mother swooped in then, straightening Avery's borrowed flannel like it was a dress. "Oh, you two look so cozy," she cooed. "Married life suits you."

Avery's face went up in flames. "Mom."

Papaw chuckled. "Sweetheart, if she blushes any harder, you're gonna have to throw her back in the snow to cool off."

The room erupted in laughter.

Somehow, Avery found herself laughing with them.

They settled near the tree for presents, the chaos swirling around her like a storm she didn't mind being caught in.

Kids shrieked with delight over toys. Wrapping paper flew. Evelyn fussed over everyone's plates. Patrice insisted that Logan take another cinnamon roll "to keep his strength up." Avery's father and Logan's brother argued about which football team would "absolutely choke in the playoffs."

Through it all, Avery kept catching Logan watching her.

Not in the heated, hungry way from last night.
 In a quieter way.
 Like he couldn't believe she was there.

When it was her turn, someone passed her a small box wrapped in simple brown paper, a deep green ribbon tied around it.

"To Avery," the tag read. "From Logan."

Her heartbeat stumbled.

She glanced up. He was leaning back against the couch, one arm draped over his knee, watching her with that soft, unreadable smile.

"Open it," he said gently.

Inside the box lay a delicate silver bracelet, a tiny snowflake charm in the center and a small engraved tag on the side.

On the back, in tiny script, were two words:

You stayed.

Her throat closed.

"Logan," she whispered, fingers trembling.

He shrugged, suddenly looking shy. "You didn't have to come here. You definitely didn't have to… put up with all this." He gestured around at their loud, tangled families. "But you did. You stayed. I just… wanted you to have something that says I noticed."

Her eyes burned. "I—thank you. It's beautiful."

She fumbled with the clasp until he reached out and gently took it from her. "Here," he murmured. "Let me."

His fingers brushed against the inside of her wrist as he fastened it. The contact sent sparks up her arm, and from the way his jaw tightened, he felt it too.

Papaw cleared his throat loudly. "Well, if that ain't a man gone on a woman, I don't know what is."

Everyone laughed again.
 Logan turned scarlet.
 Avery wanted to sink into the floor.

And yet… she couldn't stop smiling.

Later, after the presents and the chaos and the second round of cinnamon rolls, the cabin finally settled into a softer quiet. Kids scattered to play with toys. Parents tucked into conversations. Papaw snored in his chair.

Avery found herself standing near the window, looking out at the snow-blanketed fields. Her reflection stared back at her—flushed, tired, bracelet glittering faintly at her wrist.

"Hey."

She turned.

Logan stood a few feet away, two steaming mugs in hand. He nodded toward the loveseat by the hearth.

"Thought you might want to sit," he said. "You've been on your feet all morning."

She eyed the mugs. "Is that cocoa or your dad's version of 'Christmas coffee'?"

He smirked. "Yes."

She laughed despite herself.

They settled on the loveseat, shoulders brushing, mugs warming their hands. The fire crackled low, casting soft gold light across the room. It felt strangely private, even with both families scattered around them.

"You okay?" he asked quietly.

She stared into her mug. "I don't know."

"From the storm?" he asked. They both knew he didn't mean the weather.

"Something like that," she murmured.

"You're overthinking again," he said softly.

"You literally told me not to."

"Yeah," he said, lips curving faintly, "but I knew you would anyway."

Silence pressed in—heavy but not suffocating. Just… full.

"Logan," she whispered, "last night—"

"I'm not callin' it a mistake," he said immediately. "If that's what you're afraid of."

She looked up, startled.

"I'm not pretending it was just part of some act," he continued. His voice dropped, steady and sure. "It was real. For me."

Her heart thudded against her ribs. "I don't know how to do this. Any of this. My life has always been school, work, and responsibility. Now I'm here with you and our families and it feels like… like my whole world shifted overnight."

His gaze softened. "Maybe it needed to."

"And if I mess it up?" she whispered.

"Then we mess it up together," he said simply. "One step at a time."

"It's not that simple."

"No," he agreed, "it's not. But I still want it."

Her lungs stuttered. "You do?"

"Yeah." His fingers brushed hers where their hands rested on the couch between them. "I want you. I want this. Whatever 'this' ends up being."

She stared at their hands, at the bracelet glittering against her skin, at the way his thumb traced slow circles against her knuckles like he couldn't help it.

"You're stubborn," she said quietly.

"I learned from the best."

She huffed a short, shaky laugh.

For the first time that morning, the fear didn't feel quite so heavy.

Maybe, she thought, letting herself lean just a fraction closer—

Maybe it was allowed to feel like hope.

Chapter 25

Wrapped in You, Finally

By the time afternoon settled over the ranch, the house buzzed with the warm chaos of two full families under one roof. Kids raced through the halls with new toys, cousins argued over card games, and someone—probably Logan's brother—kept burning bacon even though breakfast was long over.

Avery floated between rooms, helping where she could, smiling when she should, trying her best to look normal.

But nothing felt normal.

Not after last night.
 Not after this morning.
 Not after the way Logan had looked at her before the house erupted in holiday noise.

She caught glimpses of him all day—carrying firewood over one shoulder, helping her dad hang lights on the porch, leaning in close to answer her mom's questions about ranching. Every time he laughed, her heart reacted before her head could catch up.

And every time she looked away, she could feel his eyes follow her.

The weight of it built beneath her ribs, warm and terrifying and impossible to ignore.

Logan lasted through the family chaos for as long as he could.

But sometime after lunch—after Avery had been pulled into helping the kids build a gingerbread barn, after Papaw had teased Logan about "finally settling down," after Logan had caught Avery smiling at him from across the room like she didn't mean to—

He stepped outside to breathe.

The cold struck his skin like a jolt of clarity.

He'd been shoveling the same strip of snow for minutes when—

"You look like hell."

Logan flinched and turned. Maddie stood at the edge of the porch, arms crossed, one eyebrow raised like she already knew exactly what she'd walked into.

"Jesus, Mads," he muttered. "You tryna give me a stroke?"

She smirked. "You didn't even see me walk up. That's how off your game you are."

He scowled. "I'm not off my game."

"Logan," she said flatly, "you've cleared one patch of snow three times. That's not cleaning. That's panicking."

He rubbed a hand over his face. "What do you want?"

Her expression softened into something lethal. "The truth."

He stilled.

Maddie stepped closer. "You wanna tell me why you and Avery act like you're newlyweds one minute and deer in headlights the next?"

He swallowed. "Nothing's off."

"That wasn't a denial," she sing-songed.

"Mads—"

Her voice dropped. "You care about her."

He didn't answer.

"You look at her," she continued quietly, "the same way Dad looked at Mom after he proposed. Like it was love at first sight."

Logan's breath shook out of him. He leaned back against the railing, staring at the fields washed in white beneath the winter sun.

"It wasn't supposed to be like this," he whispered. "We were just helping each other out."

"And now?"

Now.
Now it felt like his whole heart lived in the other room.

He swallowed hard. "Now I want things with her. A future I never planned for. A future she might not want."

Maddie's expression softened. "Logan… that girl looks at you like you hung the moon and every star with it. She's scared. And so are you. But being scared doesn't mean it's not real."

He closed his eyes. "It's complicated."

"Everything worth having is." Maddie nudged his shoulder. "But don't push her away because you think you're protecting her. Don't be another person who leaves her behind."

The words struck bone.

He whispered, "I'm not leaving."

"Good." She reached for the door. "Then go inside and show her that."

She paused, glancing back at him, her voice softer than he'd heard in years.
 "And Logan? You're allowed to have good things. Stop acting like you're not."

She slipped inside, leaving him breathless and more certain than ever.

He wasn't walking away.
Not from Avery.
Not now.
Not ever.

Inside, Avery was helping his mom frost sugar cookies with the younger cousins when Logan walked in, cheeks red from the cold, jaw tight, eyes locked on her the moment he stepped over the threshold.

Her breath caught—because she could see it.

Something had shifted.
 In him.
 In them.

Logan drifted toward her like gravity wasn't optional. Papaw intercepted him halfway, clapping him on the back.

"Boy," the old man drawled, "you keep lookin' at that girl like that and I'm going to be expecting babies before the spring."

Avery choked on air.

Logan cleared his throat. "Papaw—"

"Don't Papaw me," the old man huffed. "I ain't blind. I see how she looks at you too."

Avery turned scarlet. Logan rubbed the back of his neck.

Papaw wandered off, muttering something about "Christmas magic" and "a house full of children."

Logan leaned close, voice low. "You okay?"

"Perfect," she squeaked, absolutely lying.

His lips twitched.

The rest of the afternoon was a blur of family noise and stolen glances. Avery's heart felt too full, too fragile, too awake.

By sundown, she stepped out onto the porch to breathe.

The snow glowed blue beneath the soft winter dusk. Lights twinkled along the railing. The cold was sharp but cleansing.

She wrapped her arms around herself, thinking she'd have a moment alone—

But she should've known better.

"I've been lookin' for you."

His voice wrapped around her before his arms ever did.

Avery turned. Logan stood a few steps away, breath visible in the cold, eyes warm enough to melt frost.

"I just needed some air," she said softly.

"Same," he whispered.

He took a slow step toward her. Then another. Until his boots brushed hers and her heart ricocheted into her throat.

"Avery," he murmured, voice rough, "do you have any idea what you do to me?"

Snow drifted around them like quiet confetti.

"I'm scared," she whispered. "This feels like too much."

He cupped her jaw, thumb brushing her cheek. "I'm scared too."

She swallowed. "Then why does it feel like falling?"

"Because we are," he said softly. "And maybe we're supposed to."

Before she could reply, he kissed her.

Slow at first.
 Then deeper.
 Then like a man who'd spent all day trying not to.

Her fingers curled into his jacket. His hands pulled her closer until her back pressed against the porch post and winter was nothing but a backdrop.

"Last night wasn't pretend," he murmured against her mouth. "And I don't want to pretend anymore."

"Logan…"

"I want you," he whispered. "Not for a plan. Not for your family. Not for mine. For me."

Her eyes stung. "And what if I want you too?"

He smiled—soft, relieved, wrecked.

"Then we're finally on the same page."

He kissed her again, snow catching in her hair, the ranch quiet around them.

And for the first time, it didn't feel borrowed.
 Or temporary.
 Or pretend.

It felt like a beginning.

Later, when they came back inside—cheeks flushed, hair dusted with snow—Papaw winked, Maddie smirked, and Avery's mother whispered "I knew it," to no one in particular.

Logan slid onto the couch beside Avery, their knees brushing beneath the shared blanket.

"Hard to believe this started as a favor," she murmured.

Logan chuckled, pressing a long, slow kiss to her temple. "Hard to believe I thought I could fake loving you."

Her breath hitched. "Logan—"

"I'm not scared anymore," he whispered. "Are you?"

She shook her head, smiling into his shoulder. "Not with you."

Outside, snow fell softly—quiet, endless.

Inside, Avery finally felt wrapped in something real.

Something she wasn't ready to let go of.

Something that felt a lot like love.

The house eventually settled into late-night silence—muffled laughter fading behind bedroom doors, the fire dying down to a soft glow. Avery stood at the window, watching snow drift under the moonlight like silver dust.

She didn't hear Logan come up behind her.

But she felt him.

His hands slid around her waist, slow and deliberate, pulling her gently back against his body. His breath brushed her neck, warm and wicked in the cool dark.

"Everyone's asleep," he murmured.

Her pulse jumped. "Logan…"

"You keep sayin' my name like that," he whispered against her ear, "and I'm gonna forget your family is down the hall."

Her breath hitched—sharp, uncontrollable.

He turned her gently, her back now pressed against the window frame. His palm cupped her cheek, thumb stroking slow enough to unravel her. His other hand traced the line of her waist, her hip… lower.

She shivered.

"Are you cold?" he asked softly.

"No," she breathed. "Not even a little."

Logan's smile turned dangerous. "Good. 'Cause I've been thinkin' about you all damn day."

Her knees nearly buckled.

He leaned in, kissing the corner of her mouth first, teasing—his lips barely brushing hers. Once. Twice. A third time, slower, deeper, until she was clinging to his shirt, trying not to make a sound.

"Logan…" she whispered, desperate.

He groaned—quiet, rough, sinful.
"That's it. That's the voice I hear in my head when
I try to sleep."

Heat scorched down her spine.

"We can't," she whispered, but her fingers curled
into him anyway. "My family—your family—"

He kissed her jaw, slow and burning.
"They're asleep."

"Logan…"

"Sweetheart," he murmured, lips hovering just
above hers, "I'm not askin' to take you apart right
here on the window."

Her heart stumbled.

He kissed her neck—slow, slow, slower.
"But I am askin' to touch you."

Her breath came out broken.

"And I am definitely askin' to kiss you," he
whispered, "like I've wanted to all damn day."

His hand slid up the back of her thigh—just high
enough to make her gasp. Heat flooded her body,
her knees trembling as he pressed her lightly against
the window.

"Logan," she begged, "please… don't tease."

He smiled against her skin, wicked and sure.
 "Oh, sweetheart. Teasin' is the only thing keepin'
us decent right now."

She let out a breathless laugh—half frustration, half
desire.

He kissed her again, deeper this time—hungry and
slow, his tongue brushing hers in a way that made
her toes curl painfully inside her socks. His hand
slid beneath her borrowed flannel, fingertips
grazing bare skin, tracing it like he was memorizing
every inch.

Her breath caught.
 "Logan…"

"Shh," he whispered, kissing her again, lingering. "I
got you."

His fingers drifted lower—slowly,
deliberately—until she felt the faintest brush of his
knuckles against the top of her thigh.

Her head fell back against the glass.

He chuckled darkly. "Careful, sweetheart. If you
make another sound like that, your mom's gonna
come lookin'."

She slapped a hand over her mouth, breath shaking.

He kissed her palm, soft and sinful.
 "There you go," he whispered. "Quiet for me."

Her body trembled.

He lifted her easily, guiding her legs around his
hips, her back against the wall now. His mouth
claimed hers—hungry, reverent, desperate. His
hands slid under her, gripping her thighs, pulling
her closer until she felt every slow, torturous inch of
how badly he wanted her.

She moaned into his mouth.

He groaned back, forehead pressing against hers.
 "Sweetheart, if you keep doin' that—"

"What?" she whispered.

His voice turned raw.
 "I'm gonna forget what a gentleman is."

"And what would you do then?" she whispered,
teasing, breathless.

His smile was wicked enough to make her dizzy.
 "You don't want the answer to that. Not with both
our families down the hall."

She swallowed hard.

He kissed her one last time—slow, deep, unforgettable—before lowering her gently back to the floor, his forehead resting against hers as their breathing steadied.

"Logan…" she whispered.

He brushed a thumb over her lip.
 "Come to bed."

"Your bed or mine?" she breathed.

His smirk was lethal.
"Sweetheart, after tonight… they're the same bed."

He took her hand, fingers lacing with hers, and led her down the hall—quietly, carefully.

He closed the door behind them…

The moment the door clicked shut behind them, the air changed.

Logan didn't rush her.

He just stood there for a heartbeat, chest rising and falling, eyes dragging over her like he couldn't decide whether to kiss her slowly… or devour her.

"Avery," he murmured—low, rough, reverent.
 Her whole name turned molten on his tongue.

She swallowed. "Logan…"

He crossed the space between them in three slow steps, backing her gently toward the bed until her thighs brushed the mattress edge. One hand came up to cup her cheek, the other slid around her waist, pulling her so close she could barely breathe.

"You drive me out of my damn mind," he whispered, brushing his nose against hers. "All day… all night… I've been thinkin' about how you looked when you woke up in my arms."

Her breath caught.

"Logan…"

His lips ghosted hers—once… twice… barely touching.

"You want me to kiss you?"
 His voice was wicked velvet.

"Y-yes," she whispered.

He smiled against her mouth.
 "Sweetheart… I was hopin' you'd say that."

His mouth crashed into hers—deep, consuming, slow but desperate, like he'd been waiting hours to taste her again. She melted into him instantly, fingers tangling in his shirt as he guided her backward onto the bed.

He crawled over her, one knee between her thighs, his weight braced above her, warm and heavy and perfect.

When his lips left hers to trail down her throat, Avery gasped—loud enough that he covered her mouth with his hand, eyes dark with warning.

"Quiet," he whispered, breath hot against her skin. "Family's down the hall. Don't make me put my hand anywhere else to keep you quiet."

Her entire body shivered.

He felt it.

"Yeah," he murmured, voice dropping even lower. "That."

His mouth found the hollow of her collarbone, kissing—slow, open-mouthed, sinful.
 His hands slid beneath her flannel, fingertips dragging up her ribs, memorizing every inch of her.

She arched into him, breath shaking.

"Logan—"

"Shh," he breathed against her chest. "I'm right here."

His hand slipped higher—teasing her through the thin fabric beneath, not touching where she needed him most… not yet.

She whimpered.

He smiled against her skin.
 "Sweetheart, you make the prettiest sounds."

His thumb skimmed her lower stomach.
 "Tell me what you want."

"I… I want you."

"Good," he whispered, kissing her jaw again.
"Because I'm not lettin' you go tonight."

His hand slid to her thigh, gripping, pulling her closer until the heat of him pressed perfectly between her legs.

She choked on a breath.

He groaned, deep and low.
 "Sweetheart… don't do that unless you want me to forget every promise I made about bein' careful."

Her hips lifted instinctively.

He cursed softly against her throat.
 "Okay. That's it."

He guided her thigh higher around his waist,
grinding against her slow… firm… controlled.
 She felt every inch of how badly he wanted her.

Her breath hitched—loud.
 He covered her mouth again.

"Quiet," he warned softly, eyes burning. "I swear,
Avery… the things I'd be doin' to you right now if
we were alone."

Her eyes fluttered.

"Like what?" she whispered into his palm.

Logan's breath stilled.

He lowered his hand from her mouth and brought it
to her jaw, gently turning her face so she had to
meet his gaze.

"Oh, sweetheart," he murmured, "you don't wanna
play that game with me."

"I do," she breathed.

He exhaled sharply—broken, hungry.
 "Then listen closely."

His lips brushed her ear.

"First," he whispered, his breath warm against her skin, "I'd take that flannel off you. Slowly. Button by button, until you're shivering and begging me to hurry."
His hand, still resting on her thigh, tightened, a silent promise.

Avery's breath hitched. "And then?" she managed, her voice barely a whisper.
He chuckled, a low, wicked sound that sent a thrill through her. "Then, sweetheart, I'd kiss every inch of you. Starting here." His lips found the hollow of her throat, his teeth grazing her skin. "And working my way down."

He trailed kisses down her collarbone, his hand sliding up to cup her breast, his thumb circling her nipple through the thin fabric of her shirt. Avery arched into his touch, a moan escaping her lips.

"I'd take my time," he murmured, his voice thick with desire. "Savoring every taste, every touch. I'd make you forget your name."

He lifted his head, his eyes dark and intense. "I'd tease you, sweetheart. Drive you wild with anticipation. I'd make you beg for it."

His hand moved lower, his fingers tracing the curve of her hip. "I'd find that sweet spot, and I'd drive you crazy with pleasure. Until you're writhing beneath me, begging me to stop… even though you don't want me to."

He leaned in, his lips brushing hers. "I'd kiss you until you're breathless, until your legs are weak, until you can't think of anything but me."

He pulled back slightly, his gaze locking with hers.

"And then… then I'd make you mine. Completely and utterly."

He kissed her again, a slow, deliberate kiss that promised everything. His hand slid beneath her shirt, his fingers finding the sensitive skin of her stomach.
He teased her, his touch light and tantalizing, making her body ache for more.

"I'd make you scream my name," he whispered against her lips, his voice raw with need. "I'd make you feel things you've never felt before."

He pulled back, his eyes burning with a possessive fire. "I'd leave my mark on you, Avery. So everyone would know you're mine."

He kissed her again, deeper this time, his tongue exploring her mouth. His hand moved lower, his fingers finding the heat between her legs. He began to stroke her, slowly, deliberately, driving her wild with pleasure.

Avery's body was on fire. She arched into his touch, her hands tangling in his hair. She moaned, her voice lost in the kiss.
"Logan," she gasped, her voice thick with desire. "Please…"

He pulled back, his eyes blazing. "Please what, sweetheart?" he whispered, his voice a low growl. "Tell me what you want."

Her legs tightened around him.

He groaned—soft but tortured.
 "Sweetheart, if you squeeze me like that again, I'm gonna—"

She kissed him—harder, deeper, pulling him down against her.

Logan's restraint cracked.
 His hand slid under her thigh, lifting her completely against him as he lowered his body over hers, pinning her gently to the bed.

"Tell me to stop," he whispered.

"I won't."

His lips crashed against hers again, his body grinding against her in a slow, devastating rhythm that made her gasp into his mouth.

Her fingers slid beneath his shirt, dragging across his stomach, his ribs, every inch of warm skin she could reach.

Logan sucked in a breath—sharp, filthy.

"Sweetheart…"
 His voice trembled. "If you touch me like that again, I'm not stoppin'."

She touched him again.

He groaned into her mouth—broken, undone.

His body pressed her deeper into the mattress, breath coming hot and uneven, his forehead dropping to her shoulder as he tried—failed—to steady himself.

"You're killin' me," he whispered.

Her legs tightened around him.

He cursed softly into her neck, kissing her there—slow, desperate.

Their bodies rocked together, breathless and aching.

"Logan…" she gasped.

His hand tangled in her hair, pulling her mouth back to his.

"Baby," he breathed against her lips, "I swear, if you say my name like that one more time—"

"Logan."

That broke him.

He kissed her like he'd been holding it back for years—hard, consuming, hungry, a sound ripping from his chest that she felt everywhere.

They were seconds from losing every thread of restraint—

when he suddenly stilled.

Breathing hard. Shaking.

"Avery," he murmured, forehead pressed to hers, "if we go any further… I'm not stoppin'."

Her answer was a whisper against his mouth.

"Then don't."

Logan's hands found Avery's waist, pulling her closer until there was no space between them. His lips met hers in a demanding kiss, a silent promise of the night to come. The world outside their bedroom faded away, replaced by the intoxicating scent of her perfume and the feel of her body against his. He deepened the kiss, his tongue tracing the outline of her lips, coaxing them open. Avery responded, her own hands finding their way to his hair, tangling in the strands as she deepened the kiss.

The kiss became more urgent, a desperate need to connect. Logan broke away, gasping for air, his eyes locked on hers. He saw the desire mirrored in her gaze, the same hunger that consumed him. He trailed kisses down her neck, his teeth nipping at her skin, eliciting a soft moan from her. Avery arched her neck, offering him more, her fingers digging into his back.

He moved his hands, tracing the curve of her back, down to the small of her spine. He found the clasp of her bra and with a practiced ease, he unhooked it. The delicate lace fell away, revealing the smooth skin beneath. He cupped her breasts, his thumbs brushing against her nipples, watching them harden under his touch. Avery's breath hitched, her body trembling with anticipation.

He pulled away, his eyes burning with a need he could no longer contain. He reached for the hem of her shirt, slowly lifting it over her head. The fabric slid down her arms, revealing her bare torso. He drank in the sight of her, the way the moonlight caught the curve of her breasts, the delicate line of her stomach.

Avery reached for his shirt, her fingers fumbling with the buttons. He helped her, quickly shedding the fabric. He stood before her, his chest bare, his muscles defined in the soft light. He pulled her back into his arms, kissing her again, his hands roaming over her body, exploring every inch of her.

He lifted her into his arms, carrying her to the bed. He laid her down gently, his eyes never leaving hers. He knelt beside her, his hands tracing the curve of her hip, down her thigh. He kissed his way down her body, his lips lingering on her skin, driving her wild.

He moved lower, his mouth finding the sensitive skin of her inner thigh. He kissed and nipped, teasing and tormenting until she was writhing beneath him. He could feel her pulse quicken, her body tensing with anticipation. He knew what she wanted, what she craved.

He rose above her, his eyes meeting hers. He looked at her, truly looked at her, and saw the love and desire that mirrored his own. He entered her slowly, gently, savoring the moment. Avery gasped, her body arching to meet him.

The rhythm began, a slow, deliberate dance. He moved within her, each thrust a promise, each touch a revelation. He watched her face, the way her eyes closed, the way her lips parted, the way her body responded to his every move.

The tempo increased, the dance becoming more frantic, more urgent. He could feel the tension building, the pressure mounting. He looked at her, saw the moment of release approaching, and knew they were both on the precipice.

He quickened his pace, driving them both over the edge. Avery cried out, her body convulsing around him. He followed, his own release a wave of pure sensation.

They lay together, breathless and spent, their bodies intertwined. He pulled her close, holding her against him, listening to the steady beat of her heart. He knew this was more than just sex; it was a connection, a bond that went deeper than words. He kissed her forehead, whispering, "I love you." Avery snuggled closer, murmuring, "I love you too."

The world melted into heat and breath and the soft rustle of sheets…

As he kissed her—slow, deep, claiming—Logan finally understood the truth he'd been fighting since the day she walked into his life:

He didn't fall in love with Avery Collins.

He dropped.

Hard.

And he had no intention of getting back up.

Epilogue One

Six Months Later — "Sunset Promises"

The Wyoming summer stretched warm and golden across the pasture, the air humming with crickets and the soft rustle of evening wind. The stormy winter felt like a lifetime ago—replaced now by long days, gentle nights, and a rhythm Avery had slowly fallen into without meaning to.

Home.

The word no longer scared her.

Avery stood at the fence line beside the barn, a halter looped around her wrist as she helped Logan finish the evening chores. The horses grazed lazily in the glow of the sunset, their silhouettes dipped in orange and rose. Her stethoscope sat in her truck—after spending the morning at the clinic, she'd come straight back to the ranch to help Logan with a stubborn colt who refused to eat.

It wasn't glamorous.

It wasn't easy.

But being here—doing this—felt right.

Logan swung the barn door closed behind them with one easy pull. Dust motes floated in the light around him, turning him almost golden.

"You're gettin' good at this," he teased, brushing straw from her shoulder.

Avery smirked. "I didn't know being your ranch hand was part of the relationship."

"You're not my ranch hand." He dipped his head, kissing her temple. "You're just my favorite person to do chores with."

Her heart melted—again.

They walked back toward the cabin, the boards of the porch warm beneath their boots. Avery curled onto the porch swing with her legs tucked beneath her as Logan disappeared inside. The sun sank lower behind the pines, painting the sky in molten color.

The screen door creaked.

Logan stepped out with two glasses of sweet tea. His T-shirt clung to his shoulders in a way that still short-circuited her brain. His hair was damp from a shower, and the evening light carved along the curve of his jaw.

He handed her a glass and leaned against the railing—watching her instead of the sunset.

"What?" she asked, mock suspicion in her voice.

"You," he said simply. "You look settled."

"I am." The truth warmed her all the way through. "More than I expected to be."

He nudged her knee with his. "Pretty sure I said this place would grow on you."

"You said that when I was knee-deep in snow trying to pry open a frozen barn door."

"And look at you now," he teased. "Summer queen."

She swatted his thigh, but her smile softened as he sat beside her. The porch swing shifted under their combined weight, and he draped his arm along the backrest, fingers brushing her shoulder. Casual. Familiar. Home.

"Remember Christmas?" he asked quietly.

Avery's heart squeezed. "Which part?"

"All of it. You freezing your butt off on my porch. Me burning pancakes. You jealous of my sister's dog wearing a sweater."

She gasped. "I was not jealous."

"You glared at that dog like he stole your man."

"He had a better sweater than me!"

Logan chuckled, sliding a hand up to tilt her chin toward him. "And remember what you said? 'Maybe you did fool me.'"

Heat crept into her cheeks. "I said that?"

"You did," he murmured, his thumb grazing her jaw. "But nothing about this—" his fingertips brushed her cheek "—is fooling anymore."

Avery leaned in, brushing her lips against his in a soft, unhurried kiss. Slow and warm, like they had all the time in the world.

When they parted, he whispered, "You staying this time?"

Her smile was quiet, certain.

"I already did."

Logan threaded their fingers together, his thumb stroking the back of her hand.

"Good," he said softly. "Because I'm not letting you go."

The porch swing rocked gently beneath them, the last light sinking behind the mountains. And wrapped in him, Avery felt the quiet, steady promise of forever beginning.

Epilogue Two

One Year Later — "Christmas Again"

Snow drifted in slow, sparkling sheets over the cabin roof, just like the night everything changed. The porch lights glowed gold against the winter dusk, and Avery stood in the doorway, breath catching at the familiar quiet of a world blanketed in white.

A full year.

A full year with Logan Hunter.

A full year of real, messy, beautiful love.

A full year becoming a family.

Inside, the fire crackled. The tree glowed. Cinnamon and pine filled the air. Avery tied the last ribbon on a present before brushing her hands against her jeans.

Behind her, boots creaked on the wooden floor.

"You're hiding," Logan murmured, slipping his arms around her waist.

"Not hiding," she said, leaning back against him. "Just remembering."

He nuzzled her neck, stubble scratching lightly. "I remember too."

She turned in his arms, her smile soft. "Merry almost-Christmas."

His lips curved. "You planning on getting your present early?"

She arched her brow. "Depends."

Logan reached into his pocket. "Good. Because I'm impatient."

He lifted a small box into her hands. Inside lay a delicate chain with a tiny mistletoe charm that gleamed in the firelight.

Avery's breath hitched. "Logan…"

"Last year we kissed under the wrong terms," he said softly. "Wanted to fix that."

He clasped the necklace around her neck. His fingers brushed her skin, sending warmth down her spine.

"You're sappy," she whispered.

"Only for you."

He hesitated.

"And… I have one more present."

Before she could speak, Logan lifted her easily into his arms. She yelped, laughing as he carried her toward the bedroom.

"Logan! Your family—"

"They're watching a movie," he murmured, kicking the door shut. "And I owe you a Christmas kiss without pretending this time."

The room was dim, lit only by the soft glow from the hallway. Snow glimmered beyond the frosted window as Logan set her down gently on the bed.

His kiss started slow—sweet, lingering—then deepened, warm and certain. Avery tugged him closer, heart racing in the comfortable, familiar way that felt like home.

"You sure?" he murmured against her lips.

She cupped his jaw. "Always."

Later, tangled in blankets and wrapped in his arms, Avery traced slow circles across his chest.

"This is the best Christmas I've ever had," she whispered.

Logan pressed a kiss to her forehead. "Good. Because it's your first one as a Hunter."

Avery gasped softly. "You proposing now?"

He laughed quietly, pulling her closer. "No. You already said yes a long time ago."

She brushed her fingers through his hair. "When?"

"The day you stopped pretending."

Avery smiled into his shoulder, heart full.

Outside, snow drifted softly.

Inside, there was warmth, quiet joy, and the kind of love she never thought she'd deserve.

Some things weren't pretend.

Some things were meant.

And she had finally found hers.

Tanisha Pollard

BONUS HOLIDAY TEASER

Winter Wishes & Unfinished Business

The first snow of December fell soft and steady over the ranch, blanketing the world in quiet white. Avery stood on the porch beside a stack of delivered packages, breath fogging in the cold as she tucked the newest letter into her coat pocket.

She hadn't told Logan about it.

Not yet.

Inside the barn, warm amber lights glowed against the dark. Logan's laugh carried over the wind—deep, easy, the sound that had slowly become her favorite part of every day. He was helping Maddie decorate for the annual Christmas charity event, humming off-key to an old country song while stringing up garland.

Avery loved him.

God, she loved him.

Which was exactly why this letter scared her.

She heard crunching snow behind her.

"Doc?" Logan's voice was warm and familiar as he wrapped an arm around her waist from behind. "You okay? You've been standing out here for a while."

She pressed a smile onto her face, slipping her hand over the pocket where the letter rested.

"Just thinking."

"Mm." He kissed the side of her neck, slow and sweet. "Dangerous."

His teasing made her laugh, but her stomach twisted anyway.

Because the letter had come from Atlanta.

From the hospital she left behind.

The one that had suddenly, unexpectedly… offered her a position she'd once dreamed of.

Full time.

Permanent.

Life-changing.

Logan pulled back to study her. "You sure you're good?"

Before she could answer, Maddie burst out of the barn, waving a piece of paper.

"Avery! Logan!" she called. "You need to see this!"

Logan raised a brow. "What now?"

Maddie reached them, breathless, face pale with excitement—or worry. Avery couldn't tell which.

She handed Logan a flyer.

Avery glanced down.

And froze.

It was a glossy announcement from the local Wyoming newspaper:

HUNTER FAMILY RANCH SELECTED FOR NATIONAL HOLIDAY FEATURE SERIES

Filming to Begin in Two Weeks

Logan blinked. "They're—filming what?"

"Everything," Maddie said, eyes wide. "The ranch. The winter festival. The family. You two."

Avery's pulse stumbled. "Us?"

"They want a segment on 'perfect holiday couples' living in small-town Wyoming." Maddie grinned nervously. "Apparently, everyone thinks your love story is… magical."

Logan groaned. "Oh, hell."

Maddie snorted. "Oh, hell is right."

Avery swallowed hard, the letter in her pocket suddenly feeling heavier than the snow around them.

Logan turned to her.

"Guess Christmas just got interesting," he said softly.

Avery forced a smile.

But inside…

Her heart was already tearing in two directions.

She hadn't even told him the truth yet.

About Atlanta.

About the offer.

About the choice she might have to make.

And now the whole world wanted to watch them.

The wind shifted, sending a swirl of snow around their boots.

Logan squeezed her hand, warm and steady.

"You're with me, right?" he asked gently.

Avery hesitated—just a beat too long.

Logan's eyes flickered. Confused. Worried. Knowing her too well.

"Avery?" he whispered.

She opened her mouth.

But the truth stuck like ice in her throat.

Next Christmas wouldn't look anything like this one.

She could feel it.

So could he.

Book Two is coming soon.

Acknowledgements

To my real-life Logan —

Thank you for being my anchor through the chaos and my muse when I couldn't find the words. Every bit of strength, stubbornness, and slow-burn charm that lives in Logan Hunter came from you. Thank you for the long talks about ranch life, the late-night fact-checking, and for showing me what real grit, loyalty, and quiet love look like. You helped me shape a cowboy who feels real, and I'll always be grateful that you believed in this story—and in me.

To one of my best friends, Elizabeth —

Thank you for being the voice that never let me quit. You read every messy chapter, listened to every wild idea, and somehow always knew exactly what to say when I needed to hear it. Your friendship, humor, and endless encouragement turned doubt into determination. I'm forever thankful that you were beside me through every word of this book.

Tanisha Pollard

To my dad, Andy N. Pollard —

Thank you for listening to every idea, every rant, and every rewrite with patience and curiosity. You've been my sounding board, my motivator, and one of the biggest reasons this story made it past "someday." Your support means more than words will ever express.

To my family —

Thank you for your love, laughter, and quiet faith in me. You reminded me that home isn't a place; it's the people who believe in you even when you doubt yourself.

To the readers —

Thank you for choosing Mistletoe Mix-Up and stepping into Avery and Logan's world. For every woman who dreams of a cowboy who smells like cedar and sin, who carries both rough hands and a tender heart—this story is for you.

To the dreamers, the writers, and the hopeless romantics —

Thank you for believing that you can still find love in unexpected places: under snow, under stars, and under mistletoe.

Tanisha Pollard

To every reader who believes love stories can heal.

And finally, to everyone who believes that love should be a little wild, a little messy, and absolutely worth the risk—

This one's for you.

About the Author

Tanisha Pollard was born and raised in Antigua and Barbuda in the Caribbean before moving to New York at age twelve and eventually settling in Georgia. A lifelong storyteller and devoted romance reader, Tanisha writes heartfelt, sensual love stories that celebrate strength, vulnerability, and second chances—even when they come wrapped in flannel and snow.

When she isn't writing, Tanisha works as a patient care technician and continues to build her career in the healthcare field. She's also a trained chef and former Disney cook, bringing her creativity and passion for detail to every story she creates. As a woman living with PCOS, she hopes her books inspire others to believe in their worth and chase joy—no matter how many storms life brings.

You'll usually find her curled up with a mug of cocoa, reading stacks of romance novels, dreaming up cowboys with soft hearts and rough hands, and crafting the next happily ever after.